GAME PLAN

"You shouldn't play this game," Catherine said, looking down at the sea.

"Why not?" Nick said. "I like this game."

She shook her head. "It's not going to come out the way you want. You won't learn anything from me. I don't confess all my secrets just because I have an orgasm—"

"Or two."

She smiled. "Or two. But you'll never learn anything I don't want you to know."

Nick seized her shoulders. "Yes, I will. And then I'll nail you."

"No. You'll just end up falling in love with me, Nick, that's all."

"I'm already in love with you." She tried to turn away but he held her. "But I'll nail you anyway."

BASIC INSTINCT

**Sex was the foreplay ...
death was the climax**

BASIC INSTINCT

A Novel by Richard Osborne
Based on the Motion Picture
Written by Joe Eszterhas

A SIGNET BOOK

SIGNET

Published by the Penguin Group
Penguin Books Ltd, 27 Wrights Lane, London W8 5TZ, England
Penguin Books USA Inc., 375 Hudson Street, New York, New York 10014, USA
Penguin Books Australia Ltd, Ringwood, Victoria, Australia
Penguin Books Canada Ltd, 10 Alcorn Avenue, Toronto, Ontario, Canada M4V 3B2
Penguin Books (NZ) Ltd, 182–190 Wairau Road, Auckland 10, New Zealand

Penguin Books Ltd, Registered Offices: Harmondsworth, Middlesex, England

First published in the USA under the title *Basic Instinct* by Richard Osborne, based on the
motion picture by Joe Eszterhas
First published in Great Britain by arrangement with New American Library, a division of
Penguin Books USA Inc., by Signet 1992
20 19 18 17 16 15 14 13 12 11

Signet Film and TV Tie-in edition first published 1992

Printed in England by Clays Ltd, St Ives plc

BASIC INSTINCT

PROLOGUE

Music came from a gleaming CD player near the window in the bedroom, the volume turned low. Beyond the window the city of San Francisco was waking to a rare clear morning; there would be no famous San Francisco fog that day.

On the bed, a big brass bed, lay Johnny Boz—a man of wealth, definitely, and also a man of taste, but tastes good and bad. He liked art and music and casual luxury; his bad tastes were more destructive—potent drugs, a little bondage, and the wrong women.

The woman straddling his bare chest was beautiful. Her long blond hair splashed across her bare shoulders, her perfect breasts falling like ripe fruit above his face, tantalizing, just out of reach of his hungry lips.

The woman lowered her red mouth to his and kissed him hungrily, her tongue darting. He kissed back, sucking her tongue deep into his mouth. She raised his hands above his head and pinioned them. She pulled a white silk scarf from beneath the pillow and bound his wrists together, then tethered them to the brass headrail. He strained against his bonds, his eyes closed in ecstasy.

She slid down his body and he entered her, sliding deep, her hips grinding down on him. He bucked, thrusting into her, stabbing, piercing profoundly into her body, feeling her full, wet weight on him.

They were caught in the moment, trapped by the searing power of narcotic sex. Eyes closed, she reared and then pounded down, her hips impaled on him; her back arched, her breasts high and firm.

He felt his orgasm welling deep within and he threw his head back exposing his white throat, his mouth open in a silent scream, his eyes turning back in their sockets. In delicious torment he tore and strained against the silk that bound his arms.

Her moment had come. There was a slim flash of silver in her hand, a sliver of steel, sharp and deadly. Her right hand dropped fast and cruel, the weapon puncturing his pallid throat now suddenly washed red with his blood. He convulsed, shot through with the pain of sudden, violent death and the overwhelming power of orgasm.

Again and again her arm plunged to his throat, his chest, his lungs. The cream sheets turned red. He died, blowing body and soul into her.

CHAPTER ONE

The red and white beacons atop the police cars scattered on the 3500 block of Broadway, in front of Johnny Boz's Pacific Heights Victorian, flashed like lighthouses. The air was thick with the crackle and burble of police traffic, and some early risers— dog walkers in police parlance—watched like playgoers; the cops on the scene adopted the nonchalance that goes with constant, casual familiarity with murder.

An unmarked police car—with no chrome, no frills, no nothing so that it could *only* have been a police car—edged down the street and stopped by the knot of cars and cops. Two men got out and looked at the elegant facade of the Victorian town house.

The older of the two, Gus Moran, nodded approvingly. "Nice neighborhood for a murder," he said.

"We're definitely getting a better class of homicide in this city," said his partner. "It can only help the tourist trade."

The two men couldn't have been more different. Like the car he drove, Gus Moran could never have been mistaken for anything but a piece of standard-issue San Francisco Police Department equipment. But his eyes broadcast two decades worth of disillusionment. The man was tired.

His partner, Nick Curran, was younger and harder to figure. He wore a good suit, a garment just a touch too fashionable to make him as a cop the minute you laid eyes on him. But there was an edge to him, a street-smart, urban toughness, the slight swagger and confidence of a man who lived his life, day in, day out, with a gun strapped to his chest. Unlike his burned-out partner, for Nick Curran the game still went on, the rules changed daily. Most of the time the only rule was that there were no rules. The street got meaner, but Curran could still handle it. He hadn't given up, he wasn't about to—not yet, anyway.

They pushed their way through the cops by the door and into the elegant house. Moran sniffed the air like a setter and tapped the side of his nose. There was a smell in that house, one that he had encountered before—not many times before, but you had to smell it only once to know what it signified.

"Money," he said. He looked at the sophisticated surroundings: the perfect, casual, art deco furnishings, the deep carpets, the art on the walls. "Nice," he said. "Who'd you say this fucking guy was?"

"Rock and roll, Gus. Johnny Boz."

"Never heard of him."

Nick grinned. If Gus had heard of Johnny Boz he would have been very surprised. Moran's musical tastes, such as they were, ran to hard-core, Texas-swing-style country. "He was way after your time. Mid-sixties—you remember: Hippies, summer of love. You were probably in uniform then, cracking heads in the Haight."

"Happy days," said Moran.

"Boz was around then. Five or six hits. Then he got respectable—for rock and roll that is. He's got a club downtown, in the Fillmore." Nick glanced at the Picasso that hung in the hallway. "But he's definitely uptown now."

Moran led the way into the blood-spattered bedroom.

"Uptown? Not now he isn't," observed Gus.

Boz was still sprawled on the bed, a slab of meat tethered to the brass frame. It was hard for Moran to imagine a more bloody set of wounds than multiple punctures to the throat, particularly in a body with a heart that had been pumping hard with ecstasy and drugs. The costly linen was matted dark with dried blood, the mattress sodden to the springs.

Curran stared hard at the body, as if photographing it with his mind and then turned away, shaking his head, looking at the cops who jammed the room.

"A fuckin' police convention in here," he grumbled. There was a forensics team, the scene-of-the-crime boys who would pick over the room, searching and probing to the point where they could write its biography; the coroner's crew who would do the same for Boz's perforated corpse; and two homicide guys, Harrigan and Andrews. It had been their bad luck to pick up the crime in that brief gray area when they were just going off duty and Curran and Moran were coming on. A couple of uniforms stood around taking in the sights. It was the usual crowd for a murder.

Already at the scene were two other cops, not the kind who normally showed up for a homicide. Curran retreated to a corner of the opulent bedroom and scowled at Lieutenant Phil Walker and Captain Mark Talcott. Walker, Homicide Chief of the SFPD, had every right to be there—although it annoyed Curran that the death of a former rock star should draw the brass when the slaying of, say, a welfare mother in Hunters Point would not. The presence of Talcott, Assistant Chief of Police and primary political bag carrier for the mayor's office, meant that something big was afoot. Something, Nick Curran knew, that had very little to do with murder and a lot to do with San Francisco city politics.

Gus Moran, nobody's fool, glanced at the

two chiefs and raised an eyebrow at his partner. "Never get yourself murdered, Nick. You'll get no privacy if you do."

"Words to live by," said Curran.

"You guys know Captain Talcott?" said Walker to Gus and Nick.

"Sure," said Curran. "I read about you in Herb Caen's column all the time."

"Funny, Nick," said Talcott.

"What's the chief's office doing here, Captain?" Moran knew how to be polite. He was better at it than Curran.

Talcott folded his arms across his chest and his eyes swept the room, a commander of men. "Observing," he said, dead serious.

Gus Moran smirked and it was all Nick Curran could do to stop himself laughing out loud. Walker glowered at him. The look eloquently said: Don't piss off the wrong people.

The coroner pulled what looked like a large meat thermometer out of Johnny Boz's liver. It slipped out with a particularly disgusting sucking noise.

"Time of death?" asked Walker.

The coroner read the dial. "Ninety-two degrees. He's been cooling a while . . . say six hours." He glanced at his watch. "Puts time of death at 4 A.M. plus or minus."

The forensics team was unpacking a small piece of electronic equipment. It looked like a vacuum cleaner with a flashlight attached, but a flashlight that shot a thin beam of green light. It was the newest piece of SFPD razzle-dazzle, a laser scanner that would pick up every trace of human evidence in the room—fingerprints, blood, hair, skin.

"So what happened?" demanded Talcott.

"The maid came in an hour ago and found him," said Walker. "She's not a live-in."

"Nice way to start the day," observed the guy from the coroner's office.

The laser scanner was ready to run. "Could somebody close the drapes, please?" asked one of the crime-scene guys.

One of the uniformed cops drew the heavy drapes and the room darkened. The scanner wand glowed an unhealthy green and the color bounced off the mirrored ceiling tinting the cops' faces a ghoulish gray.

"So maybe the maid did it," said Gus.

"She's fifty-four years old and weighs two hundred and forty pounds."

"No bruises on the body," said the coroner.

"It ain't the maid," Gus deadpanned. "Woulda been so much easier if it was."

"Boz left the club last night around midnight," said Andrews. "That's the last time anyone saw him. Saw him alive, anyway."

"Did he leave the club alone?" asked Curran.

"Girlfriend," said Harrigan.

"Not," said Moran, "two-forty and fifty years old. I'm guessing."

Nick looked down at the body. "What was it?"

"Ice pick," said Harrigan handing Curran

a clear plastic evidence bag. It contained an ice pick, caked with blood.

"Very personal. Get in close. You'd smell him, feel him. How many wounds?"

" 'Bout a dozen," said the coroner. "Three or four superficial but eight or so—any one of them would have done it. Tied up like that, he woulda bled to death in a couple of minutes. With a dozen punctures he woulda been a fuckin' sieve. Neck like a colander, for God's sake."

"Where'd you find it, the ice pick?" asked Nick Curran.

"Nice and neat on the coffee table in the living room."

The laser picked up something on the bed, wet spots showing up like dark bruises. "There's come all over the sheets," said the crime-scene guy. " 'Bout half a gallon of the stuff."

"Very impressive," said Nick.

"He got off before he got offed," said Gus Moran.

"Coming and going at the same time," said Harrigan, sniggering.

"That is enough," said Talcott sternly. "*Gentlemen*, this is sensitive. Mr. Boz was a major contributor to the mayor's campaign. He was chairman of the board of the Palace of Fine Arts—"

Gus frowned. "I thought he was a rock-and-roll star?"

"He was a *retired* rock-and-roll star," said Walker.

"In San Francisco rock and roll is art, Gus," said Nick.

"Mr. Boz was a civic-minded, very respectable rock-and-roll star," Talcott said severely. That was true even of his club down in the Fillmore. Once upon a time that neighborhood had been home to serious jazz and hard-core rock and roll. Now it was a Yuppified district with very hip but very respectable clubs, restaurants that served the expensive cuisine of the moment, and trendy boutiques.

All of the cops were thinking that the corpse on the bed didn't look like *Mister* anything, let alone civic-minded and respectable.

"And what's this?" asked Gus, peering down at the pile of white powder on a mirror on the end table next to the bed.

"Jeez," said Curran, "offhand I'd say it looks like some civic-minded, very respectable cocaine. I mean, that's what it looks like to me. I *could* be wrong. . . ."

Talcott refused to be drawn. He spoke evenly, calmly, but there was no mistaking the ice in his words. "Listen to me, Curran. I'm going to get a lot of heat on this. I don't want any mistakes."

Mistakes, in Talcott's lexicon, tended not to mean errors of police work so much as blunders that would be politically dangerous to the department and the department chief.

"Hear that Gus," said Curran, "no mistakes."

"We'll do our best," said Moran. "Can't ask a man more than that, right?"

"Right. So, who's the girlfriend?"

"Her name is Catherine Tramell, 2235 Divisadero."

"Another nice neighborhood," observed Moran. "We're getting a very nice little tour of Baghdad by the Bay. Ooops, sorry. Forgot. We don't call it that anymore."

"C'mon Gus," said Curran, leading the way toward the door.

On the stairs, out of earshot, Gus Moran said, "Talcott's up bright and early. Doesn't usually punch in 'til after his eighteen holes."

"Yeah," said Curran, "Johnny Boz and the mayor must have been very tight."

"Nick!"

They turned to see Lieutenant Walker standing at the top of the stairs.

"What's the problem, Phil?" asked Curran. "Should we have asked to be excused? Or what?"

"You have an appointment at three o'clock. Make sure you keep it."

"Forgive me if I'm wrong, Phil, but didn't we just get a murder? Do you want me to work the case or do you want me to meet with the goddamn department shrink?"

"Keep the appointment *and* the murder. But do us all a favor—lose the attitude."

Curran grinned. "How about two out of three?"

"If you want to keep your job, Nick, keep your three o'clock. Got it?"

"Yeah, okay, I'll keep it."

"I feel better," said Phil Walker. "Maybe you will, too."

"Jeez," said Gus, "you have a gift, Nick. You bring a little sunshine wherever you go."

"You're right. Now let's make a delivery on Divisadero."

CHAPTER TWO

If you drove the length of one of the long north-south streets that cross San Francisco, you would pass through almost every type of neighborhood, the full spectrum from super rich to dirt poor. Nowhere was this more apparent than on Divisadero. At one end, down on the waterfront, you'd find bums, drunks, and addicts. Up in the Heights, in the 2200s lived the richest citizens of San Francisco.

2235 Divisadero fit right in with the rest of the neighborhood, more mansion than town house, with the same smell of money that had been so evident in the home of the late Johnny Boz.

It was no surprise to either of the cops that they were met at the door by a maid and they wouldn't have been surprised if she had directed them to the rear entrance, the one used by delivery men and domestics. The maid was a Chicana, more than likely an illegal immigrant and she knew the face of authority when she saw it. She did not look happy.

They flashed their badges. "I'm Detective Curran, this is Detective Moran. We're with the San Francisco Police Department."

Fleeting fear flashed across the maid's face.

"The police," said Moran soothingly, "not *la Migra.*"

The maid didn't look all that reassured.

"Yes," said the maid. "Come in." She led the way into the house and parked them in a living room. It was a majestic, elegant room with tall, arched windows looking east toward the blue sweep of San Francisco Bay. Curran and Moran looked impressed— murders didn't usually lead cops to such elegant digs.

A painting hung on the right hand wall and Gus Moran examined it closely, like a connoisseur. "Ain't that cute," he said. "Boz got a Picasso and this Tramell got one, too. His and hers Picassos."

"I didn't know you knew who Picasso was, Gus, never mind be able to identify one."

"It's easy," said Moran with a grin. "You just have to know what to look for. Like, for instance, a big signature. See. Down here in the corner it says 'Picasso' plain as day. It's a dead giveaway."

"Her Picasso is bigger than his Picasso," said Nick.

"They say size doesn't matter," said a young woman.

Moran and Curran turned. Standing at the foot of the stairs was a beautiful blonde, her clear blue eyes set wide. Her cheekbones would have been the envy of any fashion model. She wore a black and gold embroidered vest, tight black jeans, and black cowboy boots. She looked like the kind of woman a rock star might require on his arm.

"We're sorry to disturb you," said Curran, "we'd like to ask you some—"

"Are you Vice?" asked the woman coolly. If she was frightened of the police, then she was doing a very good job of hiding her fear.

"Homicide," said Nick.

The woman nodded to herself, as if Curran had confirmed something she half expected to be true. "What do you want?"

"When is the last time you saw Johnny Boz?" asked Gus.

"Is he dead?"

"Now why would you think a thing like that?" Gus had not taken his eyes from her face since she entered the room.

"Well, you wouldn't be here otherwise, would you?"

Score one for the chick, thought Nick Curran. "Were you with him last night?" he asked.

She shook her head. "I think you're looking for Catherine, not me."

"Ain't you—"

Nick Curran cut him off. "Who are you?"

"I'm Roxy."

"You live here? You live with Catherine Tramell?"

"Yeah. I live here. I'm her ... I'm her friend."

"Nice to have friends," said Gus.

"Where can we find your friend, Roxy?"

She didn't answer immediately, but stared hard at them. Curran and Moran could almost see her thinking, plotting her next move, figuring how to best protect herself and her "friend." There was an air of lawlessness about Roxy. She seemed the kind of person who resented giving even harmless information to the police. She was tight-lipped on principle.

"You gonna tell us?" asked Gus. "Or you gonna make things hard on yourself?"

Roxy hesitated a moment longer, then gave in. "She's out at the beach. She has a house on Stinson Beach."

"It's a big place," said Nick. "You want to be a little more specific?"

"Seadrift," said Roxy, "1402 Seadrift."

"Now that wasn't so hard, was it?" said Nick. The two cops turned to go.

"You're wasting your time," she said firmly. "Catherine didn't kill him."

"I didn't say she killed him," said Nick. "But maybe she'll have an idea who did. Unless it was you."

Roxy shook her head and sneered in derision. "Don't you think you better be going? It's a long way to Stinson."

"Yeah," said Gus, "but it's a nice day for a ride."

Gus was right. It was a nice day for a ride and a ride to Stinson encompassed a lot of landmarks and beauty spots. The Golden Gate Bridge, then past Sausalito on Highway 101 to Highway 1, the famous cliff-hugging coast road that twisted and curved north.

The town of Stinson Beach wasn't much to look at. A couple of grocery stores, a couple of bars, a couple of arts-and-crafts places catering to the tourists. The population was a funny combination of the rich, who had their Malibu-style beach houses, some hippy types hanging on to treasured but slightly befuddled memories of the sixties, and ordinary working-class folk who had been born and raised there but didn't fit in with either of the other groups.

It seemed that Catherine Tramell was one of the rich who used Stinson as a playground. The house was set back from Highway 1. It jutted precariously over the ocean, giving spectacular balconylike views of the beach and the Pacific.

Parked in the driveway of the house were two Lotus Esprits. One was a mundane black, and the other a mundane white, as if the owners didn't want to draw attention to themselves, even though they were driving two of the most exotic cars on the road.

Gus Moran looked at the cars and grunted. "Figures," he said.

"What figures?"

"After his and hers Picassos, his and hers Lotuses are the logical next step."

"Maybe it's hers and hers."

"Whatever. Anyway, it's nice to finally see someone who has a faster car than you got."

"More expensive maybe," said Nick, "but not faster."

They weren't talking about the unmarked police car, but Nick's private, off-duty transportation, a 5-liter Mustang.

The front door of the house was wide and stately. Set in it were two huge panes of glass, neither covered by curtains. Curtains or not, the privacy of the inhabitants was assured by the house's setting. Unless, like Nick, you just didn't give a damn and peered in.

The first floor of the house was open space and he could see clear from the front door through to the terrace perched above the beach like a hanging garden. A woman sat there, her back to Nick, looking out to sea.

"See anything?" asked Moran.

" 'Round the side," said Nick leading the way.

The woman on the terrace seemed about as surprised to see them as Roxy had been and about as pleased. She looked long and hard at Nick, then looked away. Her fleeting curiosity had been satisfied, as if she found the view of the pounding breakers far more interesting. Her blue eyes unsettled him. They were wide but knowing, and they had swept over his face like beams, reading him in an instant.

Like Roxy, she was blond and beautiful. But where Roxy had the looks of a model, Catherine Tramell had a less severe, more classical beauty. It was the kind of face that looked out proudly at the world from eighteenth-century portraits—a face of a noblewoman, an aristocrat. And yet, behind that patrician mien there was a subtle subtext, a smoky sensuousness, a banked fire burning.

"Ms. Tramell? I'm Detective—"

"I know who you are," the young woman said evenly. She wouldn't or didn't want to meet their gaze. She looked at the water as if deriving her composure from its tumult. "How did he die?"

"He was murdered," said Gus.

"Obviously. How was he—"

Nick cut her short. "With an ice pick."

She closed her eyes for a moment, as if imagining Johnny Boz's bloody, violent demise and then she smiled thinly—an odd, cruel, self-satisfied smile. That smile or that face, gave Gus the chills. He glanced at his partner and raised his eyebrows signaling: wacko.

Nick ignored his partner's silent opinion. "How long were you dating him?"

"I wasn't dating him. I was fucking him." Now she was like a little girl, saying forbidden words to shock her elders. Gus was unimpressed.

"So what are you? A pro?"

Finally, she turned full face to him, that same thin smile on her full lips. "No. I'm an amateur."

"How long were you having sex with him?"

She shrugged lightly. "A year . . . a year and a half."

"Were you with him last night?" asked Nick.

"Yes."

"Did you leave the club with him?"

"Yes."

"Did you go home with him?"

"No."

"But you saw him."

"I just said I did."

"Where? When?"

Catherine Tramell sighed, as if Nick's questions were too boring, too basic to bother to answer. "We had a drink at the club. We left together. I came here. He went home." She shrugged, a bit of body language that said, "End of story."

"Was there anyone with you last night?"

"No. I wasn't in the mood last night."

Nick had long ago decided that he didn't care for Ms. Catherine Tramell and whatever he might have thought about Johnny Boz or the chief of police's interest in the case, the fact remained that a man had been brutally murdered. Catherine Tramell treated this whole thing like a breach of etiquette and nothing more.

"Let me ask you something, Ms. Tramell. Are you sorry he's dead?"

Catherine looked at him, her deep blue eyes sweeping over him again, this time like one of the waves down on the beach. "Yes. I liked fucking him." Then she looked back to the water.

"And this guy Boz—" began Gus Moran.

She cut him off, holding up a hand like a cop stopping traffic. "I really don't feel like talking anymore."

It took a lot to make Gus really lose his temper, but Catherine Tramell's attitude was beginning to affect him like it had his partner. "Listen, lady, we can do this downtown if that's the way you want to play it."

She was unruffled. "Read me my rights and arrest me. Then I'll go downtown." It wasn't a dare, it was a statement of fact. Nick had the feeling that somehow Catherine Tramell would have gotten off in some weird way if they had hauled her in.

"Ms. Tramell—"

"Arrest me, do it by the book, otherwise—"

"Otherwise?" said Gus indignantly. "There is no 'otherwise.'"

"Otherwise," Catherine persisted. "Get the fuck out of here." She turned her blue eyes to them again. "Please," she added quietly.

*   *   *

There were a lot of cops in the SFPD who thought that Curran and Moran were apt to act impetuously, overreact to situations and do the wrong thing. But not even Nick and Gus would have been able to justify arresting Catherine Tramell. They had nothing: no evidence, physical or circumstantial, and no probable cause. She was such a mystery to the two cops, they didn't even have a hunch. So they did what she suggested they do. They got the fuck out of there.

They had driven a good fifteen miles back toward the city before one of them spoke. Gus said, "Nice girl."

CHAPTER THREE

Nick almost made his three o'clock appointment on time. Gus had pushed the unmarked police unit as hard as he could on Highway 101 and driven like a maniac over the Golden Gate Bridge, cursing the drivers who jammed the bridge at the Marin end and the midafternoon bottleneck at the Presidio. Still, it's a long way from Stinson Beach to police headquarters, so the clock was showing 3:15 P.M. when Nick pushed open the door of the office of Beth Garner, staff psychiatrist to the San Francisco Police Department.

"I'm sorry Beth," he said as Nick pushed into her office. "I got hung up. I made an unscheduled trip all the way out to Stinson."

Curran seemed a lot more upset at his being late for the appointment than the doctor did. Beth Garner was an attractive young woman, just thirty years old and two years into her job. Nick Curran was an old friend of hers—as a client and, briefly, a lover. Getting involved with a police detective—never mind one under her professional care—was a breach of departmental policy and the ethics of her profession. But Curran possessed an edgy magnetism, the quintessence of a policeman—the kind of attraction that had drawn her to police work in the first place.

She was genuinely glad to see him. "How are you, Nick?"

Curran knew enough about psychiatry to understand that when they asked how you were, they weren't just asking about your health. "That's a loaded question, Beth. I'm fine."

"Fine?"

"Come on, Beth! You know I'm fine. How the hell long am I going to have to keep on doing this?"

"As long as Internal Affairs wants you to," she said calmly. She was used to Curran's irritation. It was little different from the reaction of other cops under her supervision. Somewhere in the soul of every policeman there lurked a doubt about psychiatry. Somehow it was unmanly to have to talk to a shrink. Demeaning. Every day, city cops delivered headcases picked up on the streets to San Francisco General where they were held until they got shipped up to the state hospital in Napa. Or the cops heard that their collars were bound over for "psychiatric evaluation." What was the difference between a cop under psychiatric care and some whack-job yanked off Market Street moaning that he was Jesus Christ?

"It's bullshit," growled Curran. "I know it. You know it. It's harassment."

Beth Garner smiled knowingly. It was just like a cop to take cover behind a legal phrase to counter something he didn't like or even feared. "Why don't you just sit down. We'll talk. No harm in that."

Curran sat, his arms folded across his chest. "It's bullshit," he stated with finality.

"Yes, it probably is. But the sooner we get through these sessions, the sooner you'll be able to put them behind you. You know as well as I do, I don't make the policy."

"The policy is bullshit too," said Curran.

"Not necessarily."

"What's that supposed to mean?"

"Whether you register it or not, Nick, you must have undergone a degree of trauma after the . . . the incident."

"Christ! The incident! Why the hell don't you just call it what it is? The killings. The deaths. The two poor innocent tourist bystanders in their Fisherman's Wharf T-shirts who got in the way of the bullets from the barrel of a 9mm automatic that just happened to have been held in the hand of a certain San Francisco PD detective. And you want to talk about trauma? Never mind *my* trauma, what about the trauma of getting killed by a cop? Now *that's* what I call trauma."

"So you feel guilty?"

"For Christ's sake, Beth, who wouldn't?"

"That's very healthy."

"Oh, please . . ."

Beth Garner made some notes in Nick's file which was spread open on the desk in front of her. She wrote in a small, neat, precise hand.

"So—how are things?" she asked. "In your daily life? Having trouble sleeping, anything like that?"

"Things are fine. I told you . . . things are just about as fine as—"

"As?"

"As they can be when you have a job like mine and the department keeps on hauling you in and insinuating that you're as nutty as a fruitcake."

"Now you know that isn't what I'm saying to you. You do trust me, don't you?"

"Yes," said Nick Curran quietly. And he did. Not because she was a shrink with a white coat and a diploma but because whatever else she might be, or have been, she was first and foremost, a friend to him.

"What about your personal life? Anything to report there? Anything you'd like to tell me about?"

"My personal life. Oh, you mean my *sex* life. My sex life is fine." He paused and smiled. There really was no point in lying to her. "My sex life is pretty shitty actually, since I stopped seeing you. Stopped seeing you except on a professional basis." He held up a hand, palm out. "See, I'm starting to get calluses."

"That's kind of juvenile, isn't it, Nick?"

"Yeah, I guess. Sorry, Beth."

"Drinking? Are you staying away from alcohol?"

"It's been three months," he said. For a man with a heavy Jack Daniel's habit once upon a time, three months dry was something of an achievement.

"Drug use?"

"Nothing."

"No coke?"

"No coke," he said emphatically. "Beth, I'm working my tail off. I'm off the sauce— I'm not even smoking anymore."

She smiled. Not smoking for a pressure cooker of a man in a pressure-cooker job, showed amazing self-control. "How's not smoking?"

"It's fucked," said Nick shortly. He had been there almost fifteen minutes and his edginess was stealing over him. He was anxious to get away, to get back on the streets and find out who sliced up Johnny Boz. His work was as potent as any drug. "Now, Beth, would you please tell Internal Affairs that I'm fine. That I'm nothing more, nothing less than your average, healthy, totally fucked-up cop and let me get the hell out of here?"

Beth Garner paused a moment before replying. To terminate his appointments meant that she would never see him and

yet, professionally, she couldn't recommend
that he come in anymore. It seemed to her
that he was exactly what he said he was: a
normal police detective with a dirty job to
do—that is, if there was such a thing as a
"normal" homicide detective.

"I will make my report to I.A . . ."

"And?"

"I'll tell them that you're just an average,
healthy, totally fucked-up cop. How's that?"

Curran smiled warmly. "Thanks, Beth."

He started out of the office. "I still miss
you, Nick," said Beth Garner.

She spoke softly, just soft enough for him
to pretend he hadn't heard her.

Nick's bureaucratic hassles were not done
for the day. After leaving his appointment
with Beth Garner, he made his way down
four flights from the quiet of SFPD Headquarters' personnel department to the noisy
chaos of the detective bureau. It was the
usual quiet riot of ringing phones, clattering
typewriters, and burly detectives hectoring
suspects and each other. Controlling the
murder rate in an anything-goes city like
San Francisco was not the kind of job for
someone who liked a calm working environ-
ment. Normally, Nick Curran relished the
just-under-control anarchy of the bureau,
taking to the disarray and clutter as if it
were his natural habitat. Today, however,
the confusion around him was unsettling,
mirroring the disquiet he felt: the murder

of Johnny Boz, Beth Garner's obvious affec-
tion, Catherine Tramell's thin smile and
knowing eyes.

Gus Moran greeted him with more
unwelcome news. The old detective stood
up wearily when Nick appeared. "Talcott's
in Walker's office."

"Great."

"Still observing, I guess. Didn't get enough
observation done this morning."

"The man is an observing fool."

"How'd it go with the good doctor-lady?"

"She misses me."

Gus opened the door of Walker's office.
"Jeez, when *she* mates, it's for life."

The crowd in the office of the homicide
commander was slightly smaller than the
assemblage of cops that morning in Johnny
Boz's bedroom. Harrigan and Andrews were
the cover officers and had spent the day
working the phones getting background
information on Boz, his business, his
friends, and his enemies. They had also col-
lated the crime scene data and were waiting
for Moran and Curran so they could lay out
all they had learned.

Walker looked uptight and tense, irritable
from the wait for the two detectives. But as
it was he who had insisted that Curran
keep his appointment with Garner, he could
hardly complain if Nick was a little tardy.
Talcott had lost none of the button-down
cool he had displayed at eight that morning.

Nick and Gus were hardly through the

door when Walker swung out of his chair. "All right, let's go."

As if he had been switched on, Harrigan started reading from his notes. "Sixteen stab wounds to the chest and neck. No usable prints, no forcible entry, nothing missing."

"In other words," said Moran, lowering himself into a chair, "no nothing."

"Let the man finish," said Curran. He was pouring two cups of coffee from the pot that stood on a table near the window. Then he loaded one of them down with nondairy creamer and sugar, just the way Gus liked it.

"I appreciate that, Nick," Harrigan said sarcastically. "I really do." He hadn't spent all day working on this case to be patronized by the two cops.

"Any time, officer," said Nick. He set the cup of coffee in front of Gus and sipped from his own.

"There were no prints on the ice pick," said Andrews, picking up his partner's lead like a tag-team wrestler. "It's POS evidence—"

"Pee-oh-ess?" asked Talcott.

"Piece of shit," translated Gus. As an afterthought, he added, "Captain."

"The ice pick, you can buy one just like it in a thousand stores—K mart, hardware stores, Stop & Shop, even Andronico's. You could put five hundred uniforms on this and you'd never trace it."

"The scarf?" asked Curran.

"Expensive. Hermes—six hundred bucks." Harrigan shook his head in wonderment. "Six hundred bucks for a scarf. Who has dough like that?"

"Rich people," said Gus.

"Yeah, I know, but six hundred bucks. For a *scarf*?"

"Harrigan," Walker said in a "get on with it" tone of voice.

"I checked with Hermes—there's one in Union Square—they sell eight, ten a week here in the city. There's a couple of stores in Marin that carry them, too, and there's another Hermes in San Rafael, another eight or ten there. More at Christmas, they tell me. Overall, Hermes tells me they sell about twenty thousand a year worldwide. That's twelve million bucks a year, for *scarves*. Sheesh."

"We could concentrate on sales in the Bay Area," said Walker. "It's not impossible. If she bought it in, shit, I don't know, Hong Kong or Paris or something, then we won't have a prayer of tracing it."

"She?" asked Moran. "How do you know it was a she?"

"Any evidence he was having sex with a man?" Walker directed his question to Andrews and Harrigan.

The two detectives shook their heads. "Nope."

"It was a she, Gus."

"Yeah," said Andrews, "there's nothing in Boz's bio that suggests an interest in guys."

"No boys for Boz," said Gus.

"Tell us about him," said Curran.

"The powder *was* cocaine, Nick—"

Curran and Talcott exchanged glances like the crossing of swords.

"—high quality, high content. The shit was a lot purer than anything the narcs have been seeing on the streets recently. Most of the stuff coming in is low grade for crack. This is Reagan-era-the-eighties-decade-of-excess-style high quality powder."

"Some people are so old-fashioned," said Moran. "Sooo unhip."

All the cops—Walker, too, but not Talcott—had to laugh. The last trendy thing Gus Moran had done was to buy a leisure suit and that had been in 1974. He still wore it from time to time, much to everyone's embarrassment.

"Yeah," Andrews continued, "he inhaled it. There were trace elements on his lips and penis—"

"He inhaled it off his dick?" asked Moran.

Andrews grinned. "C'mon, Gus, lemme finish. Boz leaves about five million dollars, no survivors, and no criminal record except for a complaint brought against him and his band for trashing a hotel room in 1969. He paid a fine, paid damages, and walked."

"We know he liked his coke," said Harrigan picking up. "He liked his girls, he liked his rock and roll."

Nick Curran took a sip of his coffee. "He liked the mayor too, right?"

Talcott shot him one of his patented steely looks.

"Okay," said Walker, "what about the girls?"

"There were a couple, all of them groupy types from his club. His girlfriend, his steady, his chick, his woman, his main squeeze—that was this Catherine Tramell."

Talcott perked up. "Is she relevant here? Is she a suspect?"

"Nick?" asked Walker.

Curran shrugged and sipped his coffee.

"Gus?"

"I'd have to concur with my colleague's assessment of Ms. Tramell's culpability."

"Well," said Walker, "let me give you my opinion. She's a suspect."

Everyone looked surprised at that, but Talcott jumped as if he had just been given an electric shock. "On what basis?"

Walker had his own notes. "Catherine Tramell. Age thirty. No priors, no convictions. Magna cum laude, Berkeley, 1983. Double major: literature and psychology. Daughter of Marvin and Elaine Tramell."

"That's just *Who's Who* stuff," said Talcott.

"And why would she be in *Who's Who*?" asked Curran innocently. "'She's a smart bookworm. Went to Berkeley, for God's sake—good state school. Not like those elitists down in Palo Alto." In spite of himself, Talcott moved to hide the Stanford ring on his right hand.

"Not quite a woman of the people, Nick," said Walker.

"I know, I've met her."

"Did she happen to mention that she is an orphan?"

"Aww, that's so sad," said Gus. "Get's me all choked up. It really does."

Walker turned back to his notes. "Catherine Tramell. Sole survivor of the aforementioned Marvin and Elaine Tramell who were, in 1979, killed in a boating accident. Little Catherine, aged eighteen at the time, was the sole heir—to one hundred and ten million dollars."

"Whoa," said Harrigan.

The figure seemed to hang in the room for a moment.

Nick shook his head as if to clear it. "Are you kidding me? She's worth how much?"

"One hundred and ten million," said Walker.

"For those of you scoring at home," said Gus, "that's an eleven followed by seven zeros."

"I fail to see," said Talcott, "how Ms. Tramell's personal fortune makes her a suspect in a murder."

"Wait. It gets better. She is not married—"

"I'm available," said Gus. "You know there was something about that girl—made me want to take care of her. Really."

"—but she was engaged, once, to one Manuel Vasquez."

"Her gardener?" suggested Harrigan.

"Manuel Vasquez?" said Nick. "Wait a minute—we're not talking about *Manny* Vasquez here, are we?"

"The same," said Walker.

"You have got to be shitting me," said Andrews.

"Impossible," said Harrigan flatly.

"Who? Who?" asked Talcott urgently.

"Can't be," said Moran.

"They even applied for a license, in the beautiful state of New Jersey."

"Who? Who?" Talcott was squirming in his seat like someone who had missed the punchline to a joke that had everyone else doubled over in laughter.

Harrigan put him out of his misery. "Manny Vasquez, Captain, you remember. The boxer. Middleweight contender. He was a sweet boxer, great moves, great right—"

"Glass jaw," said Nick.

"I don't." Talcott looked puzzled.

"You remember, Captain. Manny Vasquez was killed in a fight, in the ring. Caused a helluva stink in—where was it?"

"Atlantic City, New Jersey," Walker filled in. "September 1984."

"I love it," said Nick. "She's got a hundred million bucks. She fucks fighters and rock-and-roll stars. And she's got a degree in screwing with people's heads."

"But none of this makes her a candidate for the murderer of Johnny Boz," protested Talcott. "There's nothing here to suggest for an instant that she had any reason to want him dead. A person's private life is their business."

"Particularly in San Francisco," said Gus Moran to nobody in particular.

"I'm not finished," said Walker.

"Oh, let me guess," said Nick. "She used to be an acrobat in the circus? No? How about she used to be a man? Had a sex change, right?"

"You forgot about her degree in literature, Nick. She's a writer—"

"Boring," said Moran.

"Not really. She published a novel last year, under a pen name. Do you want to know what it was about?"

"Wait," said Nick, "I bet I can figure it out."

"I doubt it," said Walker.

"So she published a novel," said Talcott. "There's no crime in that."

"I'm not saying there is, but the plot is, well, a little unusual." Walker paused dramatically. "It's about a retired rock-and-roll star who's murdered by his girlfriend."

The laughter stopped. "I think I'd better spend a little time with that book," said Nick.

Late that night, Nick sat alone in his apartment, doing his bedtime reading—*Love Hurts* by Catherine Woolf. Nick had already checked out the back flap. There was an author picture and a brief two-line bio: Catherine Woolf lives in Northern California, where she is at work on her third novel. Now, as he devoured page after page, he suddenly stopped reading, put down the book, and grabbed the phone. Quickly, he punched out Gus's phone number.

Before Gus could complain about the late hour, Nick said, "Page sixty-seven, Gus. Do you know how she does the boyfriend? With an ice pick, in bed, his hands tied with a white silk scarf."

Nick hung up the phone on a stunned silence.

CHAPTER FOUR

The next morning, everyone who had met in Walker's office had a copy of Catherine Woolf's *Love Hurts*. Nick had read the book the night before and wasn't sure what he thought of it. He didn't know or care much about literature. He hardly ever read anything beyond police reports and the *San Francisco Chronicle*, but he could sense the power of the writing and the unnerving accuracy of the murder sequence. A dozen times, as he read through the night, he had flipped back to the copyright page of the book. There in black and white was the hard truth: the book had been published a full year and a half before Johnny Boz's murder. Life—or, more accurately, death—imitating art.

The whole crew assembled in the conference room, including Talcott. They were joined by Beth Garner and an older man, Doctor Lamott. He wasn't part of the police force and the cops in the room eyed him warily, as they would any civilian.

Beth Garner did the honor of introductions. "Doctor Lamott teaches the pathology of psychopathic behavior at Stanford. I think it would be wise to ask him to consult with the department on this. It really isn't my area of expertise."

"Doctor Lamott," asked Talcott, as if already building a case against the expert, "would you mind if I ask you a question?"

"That's what I'm here for, Captain."

"Do you have any practical experience of law enforcement?"

Every cop in the room thought the same thing: as if *you* do. Walker looked from face to face hoping no one actually would say it.

"I am a member of the Justice Department's Psychological Profile Team," he said.

"Ah," said Talcott. "Good enough."

Score one for the shrink, thought Nick.

Walker took control. "Doctor Garner has filled you in on the basics of the case. We would all be interested in hearing what you might have to say."

"It's really quite simple," said Lamott, as if lecturing a group of graduate students. "There are two possibilities at work here. One: the person who wrote this book is your murderer and acted out the killing described in ritualistic, literal detail."

"Would the social class, wealth, prominence or upbringing of the author have any bearing on this?" queried Talcott.

Lamott smiled. "Madness cuts across class bounds, Captain."

"The second possibility, Doctor?" asked Walker.

"Also very simple—and with no basis in class—someone was deeply affected by the reading of this book and wished to act out the events described herein. This would be born of an innate desire or, perhaps, a subconscious desire to harm the author of the book."

"What about the victim? The dead guy?" asked Moran.

"He was nothing more than the means to an end. If the intended victim was the writer of the book, then the killer enacted the murder as described to incriminate her. To hold her up to public humiliation, perhaps."

"What if the writer did it?" Nick was watching the doctor closely, as if he didn't quite trust him. "What are we dealing with if the author acted out her own creation?"

The question did not seem to surprise the doctor. "In either case we are dealing with a deeply disturbed personality. It is difficult to assign degrees of evil to psychopathic disorders, but in lay terms a copycat murder is a little easier to understand."

"But the writer," persisted Nick. "What if it was her?"

The doctor was matter-of-fact. "You're dealing with a devious, diabolical mind. This book must have been written months, perhaps years before it was published. The crime was committed on paper well in advance of the actual event."

"Well, if the crime was committed," said Nick Curran, "why bother to act it out in real life?"

"Normally, that would have been enough— more than enough. Fantasy, even one committed to paper and published, usually suffices for actuality. *Normally*. But there is nothing normal about this. The crime itself or the copycat aspects of the crime."

"I'll say," observed Andrews.

"The crime was planned by the writer many months before and then she carried it out. This indicates one indisputable fact: psychopathic obsessive behavior in terms not only of the killing itself but in terms of applied advance-defense mechanism."

Only Beth Garner seemed to get this. The faces of the five cops looked back blankly at the eminent doctor. Gus Moran didn't mind looking like a dumb cop.

"Sometimes I can't tell shit from shinola, Doc," he said with a grin. "But what was that you just said?"

"She intended her book to be an alibi," said Beth Garner. "Am I correct, Doctor Lamott?"

"Absolutely," said Doctor Lamott.

"She wrote her alibi," said Gus. "She figured this out a shitload of time in advance and then one day she says to herself 'Hey, today I'm gonna go off Johnny Boz.' Just like that."

"The triggering mechanism of psychopathic behavior still requires a lot of research," Doctor Lamott said airily.

"It's actually pretty clever," said Beth Garner. There was almost admiration in her voice. "She's going to say, 'Do you think I'd be dumb enough to kill anyone in the exact way I described in my book? I wouldn't do that because I'd know I'd be a suspect.' "

"Yeah?" Nick was considering all the angles. "What if it's not the writer? What if it's someone who just happened to read the book and says, 'great idea.' "

"Then I don't envy you," said Doctor Lamott.

"Leaving aside the fact that nobody, but *nobody*, envies us, Doctor Lamott," said Curran wryly, "how come *you* don't envy us?"

"Because you're dealing with someone who is so obsessed that he or she—"

"She," said Harrigan. "I think we've pretty much established that."

"Very well," said Lamott, "*she* is so completely obsessed that she is willing to kill an innocent—or, at least—irrelevant victim in order to place the blame on the person who wrote this book."

"But why?"

"We have no idea. But we do know that you are dealing with a person with a deep-seated, obsessional hatred for the author and with an utter lack of respect for human life."

Gus Moran nodded. "Gotcha, Doc. What

you're saying is that we've got a top-of-the-line, once-in-a-lifetime loony tune, right? Either way you cut it, that's the bottom line, am I right?"

Doctor Lamott couldn't quite abandon himself to the vernacular, especially as enunciated by Detective Gus Moran. "Let's just say that you are dealing with someone very dangerous and very ill."

"A wacko," said Gus. "A nut."

"If you must put it that way," said Doctor Lamott. "Yes."

"I must," Moran said. "A nut."

"So what else is new?" Nick Curran said, thinking of those eyes.

"Okay," said Walker. "Doctor Lamott, on behalf of the department, I'd like to thank you for your assistance."

"My pleasure, Lieutenant."

"Nick, Gus. Let's go see the prosecutor."

Assistant District Attorney John Corelli, overweight and carrying along with the roll of fat, the perennial look of harassment that goes with the thankless job of ADA, was not happy to see Walker and his homicide cops. The Johnny Boz murder in all its lurid details had made the papers and the TV in a big way. And it wasn't just local. The networks and the big New York and L.A. media players were covering the slaying. There was nothing like a good murder to boost readership and ratings. And there was nothing like a good murder to make the reputation of a prosecutor—but only if he could take a plausible defendant to a jury and convict beyond a shadow of a doubt.

That was not a description of the lovely Catherine Tramell. The arrest of a beautiful heiress would turn up the media heat, but things would get hotter for Corelli, too—and he didn't want to get burned, not on this.

He was quick to brush off any suggestion that he take Tramell to a grand jury. "There's no physical evidence here," he said, running along the corridor of the San Francisco justice building. "Face it, there's no case."

Gus Moran almost tackled Corelli to get him to stop. "She hasn't got an alibi, John," said Gus, close to pleading.

"Okay. So she hasn't got an alibi. Big deal. You can't place her at the scene. Gimme a hair. Gimme some blood. Gimme some vaginal fluid. Lipstick. Anything—then maybe we'll talk. I don't even want to talk about that she doesn't have a motive."

"Kicks," said Nick. "She did it for kicks."

Corelli looked at him and shook his head as if pitying Curran. "Nick, get out of my face, please."

"If not her," said Walker, "who?"

"Luckily," said Corelli, "that is not my problem. And speaking as a lawyer, let me tell you, that shouldn't be your problem either, Walker. You have to have probable cause that it was her, not probable cause that clears every other person in the city of

San Francisco. Just because it wasn't one of them, doesn't mean it was *her*. Got it?"

"So what the fuck do we do, John?" demanded Nick.

"I don't know. I don't care." He broke free and headed for the elevator, pushing the down button as if he wanted to kill it. "Believe me, I can't indict. And even if I did, her defense would beat me to death with that copycat thing. Anybody who read the book could have done it."

"Can we bring her in?" asked Walker.

The elevator doors slid open and Corelli stepped in. "You want to put your ass in a sling, in the words of Conrad Hilton, be my guest." The elevator doors started to sweep closed, but Nick put out his hand and stopped them. All of the cops piled into the small car with Corelli.

"Conrad Hilton," said Gus Moran, "I like that. Maybe I'll use that sometime."

"I am on my way to court," the ADA pleaded. "C'mon guys."

"What are we supposed to do about this, Corelli?" demanded Nick. "Let me guess, you're going to suggest we do nothing. Right?"

"That's good for a start," said Corelli. "Then when you've done nothing about Catherine Tramell, do nothing again until you've done it ten, twelve times."

"I say we bring her in for questioning," said Walker. "We can't get in trouble for that, right?"

"Wrong," said Corelli.

"Catherine Tramell has got enough money to burn the whole department down," cautioned Talcott.

"She was the last person to be seen with Johnny Boz. That's enough for routine questioning isn't it?"

"Nick, if she was some Market Street bum I'd say, go ahead. Who gives a shit? But she's a fuckin' heiress."

"I'll take responsibility," said Walker.

Everyone looked at Talcott. "Do it, Walker. The responsibility is all yours. If you want it."

"CYA," muttered Gus Moran. "In case you don't know what that stands for, it stands for 'Cover Your Ass.' "

"I don't want it, Captain Talcott," said Walker, "but I'll take it."

"It's yours," Talcott said shortly.

The elevator hit the ground floor, the doors opened, and the group flooded out into the hallway. Corelli led the way, shaking his head. He looked like a very unhappy man.

"It won't do you any good. She'll waltz in with some superstar lawyer who'll get all of us canned for wasting the money of the upstanding San Francisco taxpayers." He stopped and jabbed a finger at Walker. "And your taking responsibility won't count for shit, Lieutenant. She will burn our asses."

"That's exactly what she'll do," Talcott said.

"No, she won't," Nick said quietly.

They all stopped in the corridor and stared at him. Nick had spoken with such authority and force that he sounded as if he knew something they didn't, as if he had a line into Catherine Tramell's thinking.

"Oh, she won't?" said Corelli. "What makes you so sure of that?"

Nick smiled, his own knowing smile. "I don't think she's going to hide behind anybody. In fact, I'd be willing to bet she's not going to hide at all."

"But how do you *know*?" Corelli persisted. "This is not a mistake any of us can afford to make—and least of all you, Curran."

"I said I would take responsibility," said Walker.

"Yeah, but on some hunch of Curran's?" Corelli couldn't quite believe that a hardworking, responsible police lieutenant like Walker could even consider doing anything quite as crazy as this.

"She won't hide," Curran said. "It's not her style. Catherine Tramell gets her kicks taking risks."

Talcott shook his head. "Then she's as crazy as you are, Curran."

"Hey, Captain," said Gus Moran, "you know what they say: It takes one to know one."

CHAPTER FIVE

Nick Curran would not have admitted it, not to Gus, not even to himself, but he was looking forward to seeing Catherine Tramell again. In the twenty-four hours since they had met, he had thought about her almost continuously. He was attracted to more than just her beauty. There was something else about her that fascinated him. He let his mind range over every word they had exchanged during their brief interview the day before. Reading her book, *Love Hurts*, had given him a window on her psyche. On the drive back out to Stinson, he found himself relishing the meeting to come, to see how she would handle herself now that authority had decided she was a suspect in a murder investigation.

The spoiled rich girl playing with fire was not a type unknown to homicide detectives. But usually when things got too hot, the rich girls dove for cover behind their families. But Nick knew in his bones that Catherine

Tramell wouldn't play the game that way, not yet, anyway. He was looking forward to seeing just how far she could be pushed—and how she would push back.

She didn't seem surprised to see them. In fact, for a split second the look on her face betrayed a touch of pleasure, as if she were thrilled that they had shown up at her door once again.

She was dressed casually in shorts and a sweatshirt, the Cal-Berkeley logo on her chest in faded, phantom lettering. She wore no makeup and her skin seemed to radiate freshness. Her eyes were clear. She had not spent the night pining for her lost boyfriend.

Nick got right to the point. "Ms. Tramell, we'd like you to come downtown and answer some questions for us."

She stared at him for a long moment, that slight smile on her lips. "Are you arresting me?" she asked.

"If that's the way you want to play it."

"Just out of interest, would it be the whole thing, the Miranda rights, handcuffs, the one phone call?"

"Just like in the movies, ma'am," Gus said.

"Will that be necessary?" Nick asked.

Catherine Tramell hesitated a moment, as if on the verge of calling their bluff. Then she seemed to think better of it. "No, I don't think that will be necessary."

"Then let's get going," said Nick. "It's a long way back to the city."

"Um . . . may I change into something more appropriate? It would only take a minute."

Gus Moran and Nick Curran nodded.

"Good," she said with a smile. She opened the door wide and beckoned. "Come in."

"Have a seat," she said, then vanished into a room just off the living room.

The beach house was a shrine to modern design, furnished with futuristic creations in matte-black wrought iron and glistening chrome.

The furnishings, the paintings were nice, but it was what was on the coffee table in front of them that got their attention. It was a pile of yellowed newspaper clippings, long articles from both major San Francisco dailies, the *Chronicle* and the *Examiner*, with headlines Nick Curran knew only too well.

DRUG COP CLEARED IN TOURIST SHOOTINGS screamed the headline in the *Examiner*. GRAND JURY SAYS SHOOTINGS ACCIDENTAL said the *Chronicle*. There were clippings from the two best-known counterculture papers, too, the *East Bay Express* and *The Guardian*. They were long articles which stated that Nick was not guilty, but only because he had been the victim of an antiquated system of mores that makes the sale and possession of drugs a criminal offense.

Nick felt as if he had been smacked square in the jaw. He could do little more than stare at his own sick story—his own face, permanently frozen in a scowl at the *Examiner* photographer who had caught him on the steps of the courthouse. Even he had to admit that far from looking like he was blameless, the picture made him look guilty as hell.

"Looks like you got yourself a fan club, Nicky," whispered Gus Moran.

"How long will this take?" called Catherine from the changing room.

It was all Nick could do to keep his voice calm. "Hard to say. Depends on what you have to tell us."

"Then it won't take all that long."

Then Nick realized that he could see her reflected in the full-length mirror standing in a corner of the changing room. He watched her through the half-open door, wondering if it was innocent or if she was deliberately teasing him. Artlessly, she stripped off her clothing and stood naked in the middle of the room, her back to him. She took the band from her hair and shook the long mane to her shoulders, then wove it into a loose French roll.

Nick stared. "You always keep old newspapers around the place?" he asked, never taking his eyes from the view in the mirror.

She took a light dress from the closet and slipped into it. She didn't put on any underwear. "I keep them around," she said, "when I think they make interesting reading."

She came out of the changing room.
"Ready," she said, tossing the brush aside.

"You know," Gus Moran said, standing
up, "we should tell you that you have the
right to an attorney."

"Why would I need an attorney?"

"Some people would feel better if they
had an attorney around when they were
being questioned by the police," said Gus.
"Happens every day."

"Detective Moran," said Catherine Tramell, "I am not some people."

"I noticed," said Gus.

Catherine Tramell was sitting in the back
seat behind Gus and he managed to sneak a
glance at her every few miles.

They had ridden a few miles from Stinson
Beach before Catherine finally broke the
silence. She leaned forward in her seat to
talk to Nick.

"Do you have a cigarette?" she asked.

"I don't smoke."

She shook her head slightly. "Yes you do."

"I quit."

"Congratulations."

She sat back, rummaging in her purse. A
moment later, she put a cigarette to her lips
and lit it, exhaling luxuriantly.

"I thought you were out of cigarettes,"
said Nick.

"I found some in my purse. Would you
like one?" She proffered the pack.

"I told you—I quit."

She smiled her knowing smile. "It won't last."

"Thanks," Nick said sourly.

Gus glanced at his partner, worried that Catherine Tramell would ignite Nick's fearsome temper. "So," Gus said affably, trying to move the conversation onto safer ground. "So, you working on another book?"

"Yes, I am."

"It must be really somethin', makin' stuff up all the time like that."

"It's a learning experience," said Catherine Tramell.

"No kidding. What do you learn?"

"Writing teaches you how to lie," she said crisply.

Oh, Jeez, thought Gus, all the ice was thin around this woman. Every word she uttered was loaded with some double meaning. "How's that? What do you mean, teaches you how to lie?"

"You make things up, but they have to be believable," she said as if she were lecturing a group of undergraduates in a Berkeley writing workshop. "There's even a name for it."

"Really? What is it?"

"It's called suspension of disbelief."

Gus laughed. "I like that." He looked to Nick. "You hear that, Nick? 'Suspension of disbelief.' I wish I could suspend my disbelief—permanently. What do you say to that, Nick? You want to suspend your disbelief?"

"It's worth a try."

"It's not as easy as it sounds," said Catherine, flicking her cigarette in the general direction of the ashtray.

They drove a few more miles of twisting highway. This time, Nick broke the silence. "So what's your new book about?"

"Haven't you heard? You're not supposed to ask an author that."

"What? Bad luck or something? I can't believe you're superstitious."

"I'm not. As it happens, it's got nothing to do with superstition."

"Then why not?" demanded Nick. "You afraid someone is going to steal your ideas?"

"No, that's not it either."

"So how come?" asked Gus, getting in on the act.

"Some writers believe that telling a plot before it is written down will lessen the freshness of the writing. It will make the plot tired and wornout before the writer gets a chance to bring it to life."

"Garbage," said Nick. "How could it hurt? You make it sound like something fragile, something that could be damaged, when all it is, is an idea in your head."

"I didn't know you were into literary criticism," she said.

"I'm not. You didn't know I quit smoking either," he shot back.

There was silence for another few miles. Then she spoke. "The book is about a detective," she said suddenly. "He falls for the wrong woman."

"Hear that, Nicky?"

"What happens to him?"

"She kills him," said Catherine Tramell quietly.

CHAPTER SIX

The interrogation rooms at the San Francisco Police Department headquarters building in the Hall of Justice on Bryant Street have all the charm of the inside of a refrigerator. The one in which Corelli, Talcott, and Walker were waiting was considered the nicest of the rooms—but the decor was still depressingly institutional. There was a Department of Public Works table, a few chairs with seats upholstered in a black vinyl, and a wastepaper basket. Set up in front of the table was a videotape camera, its lens fixed like the barrel of a gun on a single, unoccupied chair.

That was where Catherine Tramell would sit.

She entered the room, flanked by Nick Curran and Gus Moran and she surveyed the room and the men in it with a cool eye. She looked out of place. If she felt it, she didn't show it. Curran could see that masking her emotions was second nature with Catherine Tramell.

Corelli jumped to his feet as she came in and thrust out his beefy paw.

"I'm John Corelli, Ms. Tramell, assistant district attorney. I have to inform you that this session is being taped. We are within our rights to do that—"

"I never said you weren't," Catherine said.

"I'm Captain Talcott." The captain looked as if he were about to apologize, then thought better of it and contented himself with shaking her slim hand.

"Lieutenant Walker," said Walker. He didn't look apologetic and gazed at her coldly.

"Can we get you anything?" Talcott asked solicitously. "A cup of coffee, perhaps?"

"No, thank you."

Corelli took out a handkerchief and mopped his brow. The windows were sealed shut and it was warm in the room. "When are your attorneys going to join us?"

Nick did his best to hide the smirk on his face. "Ms. Tramell has waived her right to an attorney."

Corelli and Talcott looked sharply at Nick Curran. Catherine Tramell caught the glance and looked from face to face. "Did I miss something?" she asked.

"I *told* them you wouldn't want an attorney present."

"Why have you waived your right to have an attorney present, Ms. Tramell?" asked Walker.

Catherine ignored him, her gaze fixed on Nick. She looked at him with something like admiration. It was a first for her. "Why did you think I wouldn't want one?"

"I told them you wouldn't want to hide," Nick said evenly. The two of them spoke as if they were the only people in the room.

"I have nothing *to* hide."

They held each other's eye for a moment longer, then Catherine sat and looked at her inquisitors as if to say "Fire away, gentlemen." She was poised, cool, in complete command of herself. She pulled a cigarette from her purse and lit it, tossing the spent match on the table in front of her.

"There's no smoking in this building, Ms. Tramell," said Corelli.

"What are you going to do?" She raised an eyebrow. "Charge me with smoking?" In San Francisco, the nonsmoking capital of the world, there were militant nonsmokers who would not only have charged her with smoking, they would have cheerfully convicted her, and sent her to the electric chair.

Corelli, however, was not going to press the issue. He retreated hastily. Catherine blew a stream of smoke across the table directly at Nick.

Corelli decided it was time to get the show on the road. "Would you tell us the nature of your relationship with Mister Boz, Ms. Tramell?"

"I had sex with him for about a year and a half," she said matter-of-factly. "I liked having sex with him." She had complete control of the room and looked from one man to the other as she spoke.

The men in the room liked to think that as law enforcement officials, they had heard it all, seen it all, that they were unshockable. And for the most part, they were. They had heard confessions from hardened, remorseless killers, child abusers, wife beaters, hit men, and drug dealers. But they were still cops. And cops were, mainly, lower middle-class, Catholic, and conservative. To hear a beautiful, rich, well brought up, well-educated woman talk, ever so nonchalantly about her sex life was disturbing.

"Did you ever engage in sadomasochistic activity with him?" asked Corelli.

She turned her gaze to the assistant district attorney. He felt as if a lighthouse looked at him. "Exactly what do you have in mind, Mister Corelli?" she asked, ever so innocently.

Corelli shifted uncomfortably. "Did you ever tie him up?"

"No."

Corelli pressed. "You never tied him up."

"No. Johnny liked to use his hands too much. I like hands—and fingers." She splayed her own elegant hands on the dirty table top and looked at them appraisingly, as if conjuring up images of what her hands had done to Johnny Boz once upon a time and his to her.

"You describe a white silk scarf in your book," said Walker, "A Hermes scarf."

Catherine Tramell nodded. "I have always had a fondness for white silk scarves." She caressed her own wrists. "They are good for all occasions."

"But you said you liked men to use their hands," Nick said, certain that he had caught her in a lie—a small lie, a small victory.

She flashed him a smile. "No. I said I liked *Johnny* to use his hands." She stared deep into his eyes. "I don't lay down any rules, Nick." She shook her head gently. "No rules. I just go with the flow."

"Did you kill Mister Boz, Ms. Tramell?" Corelli asked in his best hanging-judge voice.

"No," she said shortly.

"Do you have any proof of that?"

"Am I required to furnish proof? I was under the impression that was your job."

"Do you *want* to be a suspect in the death of Johnny Boz?" asked Walker.

"No . . . but as to proof, Lieutenant Walker, I would have to be pretty stupid to write a book about a killing and then kill him in the way described in my book. I'd be announcing myself as the killer. I'm not stupid. Am I, Nick?"

"We know you're not stupid, Ms. Tramell," said Talcott.

"Maybe that book is what you're counting on to get you off the hook," said Walker.

"Writing the book *gives* you the alibi," said Nick.

"Yes it does, doesn't it?" she said guilelessly. She held Nick's eyes for a second, then looked down at the table. "The answer is no." She dropped her cigarette to the floor and ground it out with the toe of her shoe. "I didn't kill him."

Gus got in on the act. He leaned back in his chair and smiled affably. "Do you use drugs, Ms. Tramell?"

She was unruffled by the question. "Sometimes." She parted her legs slightly, revealing even more of her shapely thigh to Nick.

"Did you ever do drugs with Johnny Boz?" asked Corelli.

She shrugged lightly. "Sure."

"What kind of drugs?" Gus asked.

Nick was enjoying the view. She crossed her legs suddenly, cutting him out. "Cocaine," she answered Moran.

Then she smiled at Nick. "Have you ever fucked on cocaine?" The obscenity played lightly on her lips. "You should all try it. It's a nice high."

"It's a crime," Walker said dourly.

"You like playing games, don't you?" asked Nick. "That's what all this is to you. Murder, drugs. This is all just a game."

"I've got a degree in psychology. Games go with the turf. And games are fun." She lit another cigarette and blue smoke curled in the air above her head.

"How about boxing? That's a game. Was

that fun for you?" They hadn't taken their eyes off each other for a moment. Tension crackled between them like sheet lightning.

"Boxing is not relevant to this inquiry," Talcott said sternly. "Curran, you should keep your mind on the matter at hand."

It was as if Catherine had not heard Talcott. She spoke to Nick as if there were no one else in the room. "Boxing. Boxing was fun."

"That's all? Just fun?"

"It stopped being fun when Manny died," she admitted. "It's not fun, watching someone you love get beaten to death."

"I can imagine," Talcott said, with an unctuous smile.

"How did you feel when I told you Johnny Boz had died?" Nick asked softly.

"I felt as if somebody had read my book and was playing a game."

"I thought you liked games."

She shook her head slowly. "Not that kind."

Nick leaned in, his eyes boring into hers. "It didn't hurt, though, did it? It was the game that worried you."

"No. I wasn't hurt by Johnny's death."

"Because you didn't love him?"

She nodded curtly. "That's right."

Their eyes were locked now, as if they were trying to see into each other's skulls. "And yet you were fucking him—"

"Love has nothing to do with pleasure, Nick. You can always get the pleasure.

Didn't you ever fuck anyone when you were married, Nick? Other than your wife, that is."

There was a moment, a long moment of silence. Nick stared at her expressionlessly.

"How did you know Detective Curran was married?" Walker asked the question that they all wanted answered.

She was blasé, brushing off the query. "Maybe I was guessing, Lieutenant. What difference does it make?" She drew heavily on her cigarette. "Would you like a cigarette, Nick?"

Corelli shook his head. "Do you two know each other or something? Because if you do, then Nick, you have got to get out of here."

Nick's eyes never left her face. "Don't worry about it, John. We don't know each other. Do we, Ms. Tramell?"

"No," she said.

"How did you meet Johnny Boz?" Walker was all business. You could hear the determination in his voice to diffuse the electrical charge between Nick Curran and Catherine Tramell.

"I wanted to write a book about the murder of a retired rock star. I went down to his club and picked him up. Then I had sex with him." She smiled brightly at Walker. "It was as simple as that."

"I see."

"Do you?"

"You didn't feel anything for him. You just had sex with him for your book?"

Nick wondered if Boz had known that he was nothing more than research.

"That's how it was in the beginning. Then . . ."

"Then?"

"Then I got to like what he did for me."

"That's pretty cold, ain't it, lady?" said Gus.

Catherine Tramell smirked. "God, who'd have thought that a bunch of cops would be such romantics. Sex without love is a crime in your book, is that it? People use people every day, Gus, I'm surprised you're surprised."

"Use them, then throw 'em away. That your MO, lady?"

"I'm a writer," she said coldly. "I use people for what I write. Let the world beware."

"Too late for Johnny Boz," observed Gus. "Too late for him to cover his ass."

Catherine looked at the cops and the prosecutor. "You really think I did it, don't you? Never mind that I would never be so crazy as to copy a murder I wrote, never mind that you think I'm a cold, heartless bitch and why would someone like that commit such a *passionate* crime. You really think I killed Johnny." She shook her head, amazed. "I guess I'll just have to prove it to you."

"How do you propose to do that?" Corelli asked.

"Easy."

"How easy?" asked Nick.

"I'll take a lie detector test."

*   *   *

It would have been easy to mistake the polygraph cubicle at police headquarters for a gas chamber. It was a tiny, windowless cubicle, furnished with a single chair that stood alongside the faintly menacing polygraph machine. Hidden in the wall of the cell-like cubicle was the lens of a video monitor which transmitted Catherine Tramell's image into a small viewing room. She was tethered to the machine, straps and sensors snaking from the equipment and wrapping around her arms and chest like tentacles.

Although the camera was well hidden in the cinderblock wall, she seemed to know exactly where it was. She gazed at the lens, as if trying to stare down the camera. The cops had watched her bravura performance on the polygraph, with the rapt attention of first night theatergoers.

The polygraph examiner, the expert who administered the test, was impressed as well. He came into the viewing room with her responses, shaking his head. "No blips, no blood pressure variations, no pulse deviation, no nothing. Either she's telling the truth or I've never met anyone like her."

Talcott looked relieved and allowed himself the luxury of little sneer of victory directed mainly at Nick. But he saved a little for Walker and Gus Moran as well. "Then I guess that settles it," he said.

Nick peered at her image on the monitor. "She's lying," he stated flatly.

Talcott stopped at the door. "Curran, for Christ's sake."

The polygraph examiner was even more adamant. "Forget it, Nick. You can fool me, you can fool you. But you can't fool the machine. A beautiful chick doesn't turn the machine's head, you know what I'm saying?"

Nick shook off the objection. "You can fool the machine."

"If you're dead, maybe—"

"Trust me. It can be done."

"And what makes you such an expert all of a sudden?"

"I know people who've done it."

"Like who, for instance."

"A guy I knew once," said Nick heading for the door of the viewing booth.

"Yeah," said the examiner, "I'd like to meet him sometime."

"Sometime," said Nick.

Talcott was doing a fast repair job on the department's image. He stood with Catherine Tramell in the corridor of the police building, apologizing as sorrowfully as he could for having brought her in. Catherine wasn't paying much attention. She smiled a faraway smile, as if she were a monarch and Talcott a very minor official in some far-flung colonial post.

Just as Walker, Moran, and Nick Curran reached them, Talcott was saying, "Of course,

if it had been up to me—" He broke off
hastily.

Walker too, felt that apologies were in
order. "Thanks for coming in, Ms. Tramell.
I hope we haven't inconvenienced you too
much."

Catherine smiled thinly at him. "I enjoyed
it. Can I ask one of you gentlemen for a
ride?" She looked at Nick as she spoke.

"Sure," he said.

"Thanks."

Talcott, Walker, and Gus Moran watched
them go. "That," commented Moran, "is
trouble looking for a place to happen."

"Walker," said Talcott curtly. "See that
trouble doesn't happen. Anywhere. Got it?"

Walker got it.

Nick's car, a mean-looking gray and ma-
roon Mustang convertible, was parked at the
curb in front of the Hall of Justice. He
gunned the car into traffic and took off fast
down Bryant Avenue.

Catherine Tramell yawned and stretched
in the soft leather bucket seat, flexing like a
cat. The corners of her eyes drooped ever so
slightly in fatigue.

Nick shot her a sideways glance. "Rough
day?"

She shook her head. "Not really."

"Fun?"

"In a way."

"I'll bet. Beating that machine can't be
easy, but I'll bet you just looked upon it as

if it were another game. And we all know
how much you like games, don't we?"

She looked at him for a fleeting moment,
engaging his eyes, then looked away. "If I
were guilty and I wanted to beat the machine
it wouldn't be all that hard."

"No?"

"No. It wouldn't be hard at all."

"Why not?"

"Because I'm a liar. An accomplished
liar."

Nick got the feeling that, right then, Catherine Tramell was telling the absolute truth.

"I'm a professional liar," she continued.
"I spend my whole life perfecting my lies."

"What for?"

"For? For my writing, of course."

A giant, sixteen-wheeled truck zoomed by,
the driver as unconcerned by the inclement
weather as Nick was, throwing up a great
gout of water which slapped across the Mustang's windshield. For a moment it was as
if they were in a car wash, the entire win-
dowshield awash in muddy water. For sev-
eral seconds, Nick couldn't see a thing, but
he never took his foot off the accelerator.
The situation didn't seem to faze Catherine
Tramell either.

"I love the rain," she said, as if she were
on her balcony at Stinson. "Don't you."

"Not particularly," said Nick.

"You took a polygraph after you shot those
two people, didn't you?"

"Yeah."

"You beat the machine didn't you? That's how you know it can be done."

"Let's just say I passed. With flying colors."

"You see," she said with a smile, "we're both innocent, Nick."

Nick directed the car up into Pacific Heights, taking the long way along Broderick. The rain was still teeming down when he stopped in front of her house on Divisadero. The white Lotus was parked in the driveway. Nick rolled to a stop at the curb and killed the engine. The only sound was the rain thrumming on the roof.

"You seem to know an awful lot about me," he said.

"*You* know all about *me*," she said, as if the details of her sex life had been beaten out of her, rather than offered casually, almost offhand.

"I don't know anything that isn't police business," Nick said defensively.

"Oh?"

"Yeah. Oh."

"It's police business to know that I don't like to wear any underwear? You know that, Nick. *They* don't."

"I'm sure Captain Talcott would be interested to know that," he said. "Hell, all the guys down at headquarters should know. I'll add a note to your file."

"You do that." She slipped off her shoes and opened the door. "It's been fun," she said, as if this were the end of a date. "Thanks for the ride."

She slammed the door and ran barefoot through the puddles and the rain, her hips swinging. He sat behind the wheel and stared at her, his eyes on her until the moment she opened the door to her house and vanished inside.

CHAPTER SEVEN

The Ten-Four was a bar on Bryant Street, a few blocks from the Hall of Justice and police headquarters and was much favored by members of the SFPD. It was a police bar, but like the San Francisco Police Department itself, it was in transition. Once it had been a typical big-city cop watering hole—you could find the equivalent in New York, Detroit, Chicago, Boston—anywhere the police were enclaves of second and third generation immigrants, conservative law-and-order hardliners. Hard drinks, served in a place with no atmosphere, with a kitchen that was a shrine to deep frying and grease.

But the makeup of the SFPD was changing. The older, old-fashioned cops were retiring, the newer breed was coming up. So the Ten-Four served margaritas and designer beers as well as Bud and boilermakers. The Looters, the Movie Stars, Chris Isaak—hip San Francisco rockers—jostled

Frank Sinatra and Tony Bennett on the jukebox. There was even a fern.

And there were cops. Old cops like Gus Moran and others of his ilk and wiseasses like Nick Curran in good suits and expensive haircuts. Walker and Gus Moran were seated at a back table, nursing their drinks and waiting for Nick. He hadn't said he'd be in, but they knew he would show up eventually, just like a pigeon heads for home.

Walker started in on him, even before Nick had a chance to get past the bar. "Jeez, Curran, what the hell is it with all this 'Nick' stuff? 'Nick would you like a cigarette? Nick, can you give me a ride?' Give me a fuckin' break, please."

"She didn't ask *me* for a ride. She asked anybody," Nick said defensively.

"Hey, Nick," asked the bartender. "The usual? Perrier, slice of lime?"

"Double Black Jack, rocks, Chuckie," replied Nick.

"What you doin', sonny?" Gus asked.

"It's my first drink in three months. That okay with you?"

"No," said Gus Moran.

"Too bad."

"You know her, don't you, Nick," said Walker.

"I don't know her. She doesn't know me. I never heard of her, never saw her before Gus and I talked to her yesterday. Right, Gus?"

"How the hell should I know?"

Chuckie, the bartender, placed a generous beaker full of scotch on the bar in front of Nick.

"Thanks, Chuckie. Be a pal and run me a tab, would ya?"

"Sure thing, Nick."

As they walked to a table, Curran took a deep gulp, slugging back half the scotch in one swig. He exhaled in satisfaction and licked his lips. It tasted good. Too good. It tasted ever so faintly like danger.

"Tell me again, Nick," said Walker. "Just reassure me. You do not know Catherine Tramell except in the line of duty?"

"Right."

Walker's eyes narrowed in suspicion. "You sure?"

"I'm sure." He swigged the strong brown drink as if he needed it to get through the next few minutes of his life. "So tell me. Now what?"

"What now what? It's over. It's over as far as she's concerned. Stay away from her, Nick. Do yourself a favor. Do us all a favor. You think I enjoy having Talcott breathing down my neck? Think again."

"You're letting her walk, just like that?"

"What am I supposed to do? She passed the polygraph with flying colors, Nick. Personally, I'm delighted. No more Catherine Tramell. Thank God." Walker took a sip of his own drink, a vodka tonic. He seemed to need it just as much as Nick. His higher rank did not insulate him from dangers of alcoholism—quite the opposite.

"She passed the polygraph. For Chrissake, she didn't *pass* the test, she *beat* the machine. That's why she asked to take it."

"How the hell do you know?" Gus Moran almost bellowed at his partner. "What is it with you and this broad anyway, Nick? Take it from me, you're too old to go girl crazy."

"She's just another suspect," muttered Curran.

"Christ," said Moran, "I don't know whether to laugh or cry."

"She's a former suspect," corrected Walker, "who just happened to pass the polygraph. Enough. That's all she wrote. End of story."

"But maybe that isn't all she wrote."

"Please, Nick, please," groaned Walker.

"Come on, Phil, you're not going to let this slide, are you? What about her parents? What about what else she published? Maybe *all* her books have a way of coming true."

Phil Walker shook his head slowly. Suddenly he looked tired, drained and older than his forty-five years. "Her parents died in an accident. I don't care what else she's written. And what the fuck are you—a book critic all of a sudden?"

"How did they die?" Nick persisted, like a fighter trying to wear down his opponent. "Was there an investigation?"

"I can't figure you, Nick," said Moran. "And I thought I pretty much had you fig-

ured out. You got a hard-on for her body or
you got a hard-on for nailing her for murder? One minute I think it's just her bod,
the next I think you think she's fuckin' Al
Capone, Public Enemy Number One. Or is
it both?"

"And now you're saying maybe she killed
her parents. Let me guess, you think she
killed Manny Vasquez, too, right?"

"Yeah," said Moran. "She got up in the
ring and turned into one mean sonofabitch."

"Maybe, just maybe, Gus," said Walker.
"Maybe she grew herself an Afro and learned
a left hook that could kill a man and put
shoe polish on her face. Let's polygraph her
again and ask her about it."

"Fuck you, Phil," said Nick casually.

"Hey, while we're on the subject, Nick,
fuck you, too."

"I feel left out," said Moran, ruefully.

"Your turn will come," said Nick. He
drained his drink and waved the empty
glass at the bartender. "How about another
double Black Jack there, Harry?"

"Sure thing, Nick," said the bartender.

"C'mon, Nick," said Moran, his brow
creased in concern. "You don't need that
shit."

"You need it," countered Curran. "Phil
needs it. Every cop in this joint needs it."

Harry, the bartender, didn't deliver the
tall, potent drink to Curran's table. Instead,
a florid man with thinning hair and a suit
that made Gus Moran look as if he had just

stepped from the pages of *GQ* set the glass down in front of Nick. He was slightly glassy-eyed with his own spirited imbibing and he swayed as he stood over the table. "There you go, Shooter," he said with a malevolent grin. "Drink up. Back on the Black Jack, huh, Shooter."

Nick took the drink but didn't look up at his tormentor.

"We're discussing a case, Marty," said Walker quietly and firmly.

Marty Nilsen, Internal Affairs investigator and no friend of Nick Curran's, assumed an exaggerated air of grievance. "I know that. I had absolutely no doubt about that. Really. So discuss." He shoved the drink a little closer to Nick, taunting him. "Drink. Drink your double, Shooter."

Gus Moran, sitting next to Nick Curran, could feel his partner go taut, tense like sprung steel, ready to lash out at the beefy IA investigator. Nick's hands curled into hard fists. Moran put a hand on his forearm, ready to pull his partner back should he decide to strike.

Curran swallowed hard, barely restraining himself. "I'm off-duty, Nilsen," he said, fighting to control the anger in his voice. "You hear that? I'm off-duty and I'm discussing a case with my partner and my division chief. Internal Affairs shouldn't have any trouble with that. Maybe I should put in for a little overtime. What do you say?

Think the shooflies will have any trouble with that?"

"Hey, Shooter, I don't have any trouble with it. But don't work *too* hard. It might drive you to drink."

A cold gust of wind blew through the bar as Beth Garner pushed into the room from the rain-lashed street. She arrived at the Ten-Four just in time to see Nick lose control—almost. Nick was on his feet, Walker and Moran trying to pull him back down to the table.

"Stop riding me, Nilsen," Curran yelled, "or so help me I'll ram your fuckin' teeth down your throat."

"Hey, hey, what's the problem?" One-hundred-and-two-pound Beth Garner got between the two tough cops. "Let's simmer down."

"No problem, Doc," said Nilsen with a sneer. "No problem now that the headshrinker is here just in time to save her favorite patient." He enveloped Beth Garner in a sweaty, boozy, bear hug.

She shook him off. "Fuck off, Marty."

Nilsen was either very drunk or unusually thick-skinned, even for an Internal Affairs cop. "You kids have a good time," he said with a hearty laugh and then staggered away.

Nick, however, was slower to cool down. He watched the cop cross the room. His eyes blazed, boring into his back like knife points. "He's asking for it. And I'm just in the mood to give it to him."

Beth pulled him back to the table. "Sure, that's the way, play into his hands. He's asking for it. But don't take the bait, Nick. Don't give him the satisfaction."

Curran took a deep breath, as if that alone could quell the fire of his anger. But he realized he needed more. "You want to get out of here?" he asked.

"Yes," Beth said. She hooked her arm into his, an affectionate and proprietary gesture.

"Good." He turned back to Walker and Gus Moran, tossing some bills on the table. "Take care of my tab, Gus," he said. "And have one on me." Nick Curran steered Beth Garner toward the exit and the rain-swept streets.

The two cops watched them leave, then turned back to their drinks. "Don't they make a lovely couple?" said Gus.

"I thought it was over between them."

"Well, maybe not tonight. Maybe tonight it's just for old times' sake."

"Sometimes I think he started banging her just to get himself off the hook with Internal Affairs."

"Naw," said Gus. "He ain't like that. My partner's got heart."

The rage that had built up in Nick Curran that day boiled over the moment he and Beth got into her apartment. As she started to turn on the lights he reached for her, grabbing her, and kissing her urgently, hungrily, pushing her up against the door. He was hard and rough and a wave of fear washed through her body. She tried to push him away and felt his mean determination that she would submit.

"Don't—please, Nick—"

His answer was inarticulate but plain. He dug his hands down into her dress and the cloth parted with a wrathful tearing; a hot hand slid up her cool thigh to her panties, his nails scrabbling at the filmy fabric. He pulled the dress off her shoulders and then pushed his hands under her bra, scooping out her breasts.

Her voice was shot through with panic. "Please don't—don't—"

He lowered his mouth to her shoulder and with a snarl he bit her skin, pulling her to the floor.

He raised himself above her long enough to open his shirt and push down his pants, thrusting enraged into her. Beth Garner had no deeply hidden fantasies of rape. She felt not a flicker of desire for Nick, but a sickening disgust and a building hatred.

He thrust and bucked and lunged, as if the mere force of his ardor could soothe the pain he had caused her, as if he could somehow force her to experience pleasure. But the torment and punishment he meted out with his body far outstripped any gratification. She could only wait until he finished and hope he would not harm her any more than he had already.

He came quickly, the sperm pumping out of him, leaving him spent but with a buzzing in his brain and a blurry dissatisfaction, his hunger and his need unslaked.

Curran rolled off her and lay by Beth's side staring at the ceiling. Now that it was done, she felt no fear of him, nor hatred, just a pathetic pity. She touched the bruise on her shoulder and sat up, unable to look at him.

He put out his hand to touch her, to reassure her if he could, but she refused to be comforted. She brushed him away and shivered.

"Beth . . ."

"What was she like?" Beth Garner was a psychiatrist and she knew her way through the rocky terrain of Nick Curran's psyche. This was not about her, Beth Garner. She was nothing more than an innocent bystander.

"Who?"

"Catherine Tramell."

"What makes you think I'd know what she's like?"

"I know you don't know what she's like in bed, Nick, otherwise this wouldn't have happened."

"Beth—"

"No, I'm talking about Catherine Tramell's other performance."

Nick was silent a moment. "You had her pegged," he said softly. "She used the book as her alibi."

He sat up and kissed her shoulder where he had bitten it a few minutes before. She did not move. It was like kissing marble.

"I met her at Berkeley," she said.

"What?"

"We were in some of the same classes." She smiled ruefully over her shoulder. "Psych, you know. We have that much in common or didn't it occur to you?"

"It didn't." Beth and Catherine Tramell were about the same age. They had both been psych majors at Berkeley at about the same time. "It should have."

"You haven't been thinking much about me, Nick. Not for a long time. And less in the past few days."

"Why didn't you tell me you knew her?" She looked at him sharply. "I'm telling you now."

"You took your time."

"Well, you didn't. I would have made love with you, Nick. I *wanted* to—but not like that. You've never been like that before." She stared hard at him as if straining to read his face in the half light. "Why, Nick?"

"*You're* the shrink," he said callously.

She stood and gathered her tattered dress around her bare shoulders. "Yes, I'm the shrink, but you weren't making love to me."

"Well, then who was I making love to, Doctor Garner?"

"You weren't making *love*, Nick."

"I need a cigarette," he said.

"I thought you quit."

"I started again."

"You'll find some cigarettes in the top drawer. In the foyer," she said harshly. "Get them on your way out."

CHAPTER EIGHT

The bars close at 2 A.M. in San Francisco and that gave Nick Curran almost three hours to smoke a pack of cigarettes and get through most of a fifth of Johnnie Walker Black in some dump of a place in the Mission. When that closed, he hit an after-hours place South of Market for a couple more shots and when that dive closed, he managed to get home and sleep a drink-sodden couple of hours. He awoke with a headache that felt like someone had stuffed a sea anchor into his brain and with a tongue which seemed to be upholstered in fake fur. He could cope with the hangover—he had had them before—but the hatred he felt for himself ground at him.

By the time he got to headquarters, the entire Johnny Boz task force had been assembled in Walker's office for a couple of hours. No one stood on ceremony.

"You look like dogshit," said Walker.

"I've seen dogshit that looked better," said Andrews.

"Boz looked better," Harrigan said.

"Don't pay any attention, sonny," said Gus with a shit-eating grin. "You don't look that bad. You just look a little headshrunk is all."

"Everybody is a fuckin' comedian," growled Nick. He poured himself a steaming mug of coffee and drank it as eagerly as he had the scotch the night before. "We got anything?"

"I made some calls over to Berkeley," said Andrews. "There was a murder in '77. A professor—ice pick, in his bed, multiple stab wounds."

Nick Curran smiled thinly. "And our girl was there then, wasn't she?"

"University records say she was," Andrews said.

"Wait," said Nick. " '77? What is she now? Thirty? Thirty-one? In 1977, she would have been—" he did some fast mental arithmetic, no mean feat, considering how he felt right at that moment. "Sixteen? Seventeen?"

"So, she was a fuckin' child prodigal," said Moran.

"Gus, I know your dumb-shit act is just an act," said Nick, "but these guys don't."

"So," said Walker, "are we saying that some sixteen-year-old coed ice-picked to death a college professor?"

"We're talking about Catherine Tramell," said Nick. "Not just any sixteen-year-old coed. I wouldn't put it past her."

"We'll have to check it out." Walker did

not sound happy. "Gus, head over to Berkeley, see what you can find out. Harrigan, find out what else she's published. Andrews, get the files on the accident, her parents' accident. And everyone copy Beth on everything. I want psychological input on this one. Got it?"

"What about me?" demanded Nick.

"You're already getting psychological input, son," said Gus Moran, sniggering.

"The first thing you can do, Nick, is go stick your head in a bucket of ice water. Then follow her. See if she leads us anywhere."

Nick didn't bother with the ice water, but he picked up a few cups of coffee at a 7-Eleven and drank them as he drove out to Stinson Beach. He rolled down all the windows in his unmarked car and let the wind buffet his face. The Golden Gate was shrouded in fog, but the tang of the salt air on the bridge whipped away the alcohol cobwebs in his brain; he felt about eighty-five percent human by the time he made it to Stinson.

The black Lotus was parked in front of the house and he spent a long hour waiting for her to emerge and climb into the machine.

She drove well, but she didn't blast off out of her driveway. Nick smiled to himself—sometimes even Catherine Tramell didn't bother to live life in the fast lane. Nick hung back on Highway 1, a safe distance, giving her a long lead, keeping her just in sight. Better to lose her than to have her make the tail.

A moment later he was furious at himself for his complacency. Suddenly, she floored her accelerator and the powerful car seemed to jump forward on the road, like a race-horse being shown the whip hand.

She wove through traffic, cutting in and out of the line of cars, passing on the left and right, doing anything it took to get ahead on the curving road. Nick wiped the sweat from his upper lip and took off after her, pushing, urging his car to keep up with her.

The tourists on Highway 1 out for a sedate morning drive were just getting over the shock of seeing a Lotus pass them at warp speed when a dirty, brown Chevrolet blew by them doing the same kind of free-way gymnastics.

But the recklessness Nick had already witnessed was nothing but an overture for her next automotive trick. She pointed the Lotus into a blind curve, aiming for the inside as if she were alone on the road, blocking the left lane completely. Nick was right with her, on the left, three cars back; then she sliced back into the line of cars, taking her place on the right like a law-abid-ing motorist—and revealing to Nick a huge Gray Lines tour bus barreling toward him like an artillery shell.

There was a car on his right, a sheer cliff

on his left. There was no place to go but
right at the bus and hope he could edge back
into traffic before being smashed into a
highway statistic. He floored the gas pedal
and wrung a few last horses out of the
screaming engine. The bus blasted its horn
and kept coming. The car on the right
stayed close. He was trapped.

In a split second he made his decision:
He slammed on his brakes and skidded back
into the right lane—his bumper almost
stuffed into the trunk of the car in front of
him—edging out of the way of the bus
which roared by, horn blaring.

"Fuck it!" Nick pounded the wheel. It
was either lose the tail or get killed. *Now* it
was time to get back on Catherine Tramell's
trail. Frazzled though he was by the close
call, he stamped the accelerator down to the
floor and pulled into the left lane again, racing after her.

Far ahead of him, he saw a low-slung
black shape: the Lotus, taking the exit for
Mill Valley. He breathed a little easier. Mill
Valley was a small, quiet, rich little town.
The local cops weren't going to let a black
Lotus get away with playing highway tag,
not in their nice neighborhood.

He caught up with her in the hills above
the town, trailing her through the narrow,
winding streets running through the ter-
raced slopes of the hillside. She stopped in
front of a nondescript house, an almost tumbledown place, poor and at odds with the

solid middle-class homes on either side of it on a sunny street called Albion Avenue. He made a note of the number.

Catherine Tramell parked and shut down the Lotus, then darted for the front door of the building and was inside by the time he drove by slow and sedate. He parked a few cars down the street and settled in for a wait.

After an hour, he was bored rigid. Just for something to do, he got out of the car and surveyed the house. He could see nothing, certainly not in the windows. He opened the battered letterbox and found a piece of mail that announced that Ms./Mr. Hazel Dobkins (or current occupant) may have already won one million dollars! The envelope also advised that Ms./Mr. Hazel Dobkins should look inside the envelope immediately for information concerning the claiming of her Valuable Free Gift!

The name meant nothing to him. It was dark by the time Catherine Tramell emerged from the house with a frail woman somewhere in her middle sixties, and he could only make an educated guess as to Hazel Dobkins's identity: a family member, an aunt perhaps, or maternal grandmother. The ages jibed, but Catherine Tramell just didn't seem like the type who would be big into family.

She slipped into the Lotus and drove away from the house, taking the hill road down to the valley floor. She didn't seem to be in a hurry—not, that is, until she reached the outskirts of the town of Mill Valley.

She was approaching a traffic signal, serene and stately like a driver with an unblemished record. A car stood at the intersection, waiting for the light to change. Catherine advanced on it, the Lotus engine growling like a jungle cat.

Then, suddenly, she gunned the motor and the car jumped, heading straight for the impossibly narrow space between the car and the curb. At full speed, she sliced between them—scaring the hell out of the driver—and turned a sharp right into the intersection just as the light changed to green.

Nick was after her, but he was a split second too late. The suburban motorist, startled like a spooked horse by the careening Lotus, swerved into his path. He stood on his brakes and screeched to a halt.

He pointed his car toward Stinson, almost convincing himself that he was headed there on routine police work. He told himself he was following Walker's orders, that, for once, he was doing what he had been told to do by a superior. But much as he hated to admit it, he knew the truth: He had to see Catherine Tramell again.

The black Lotus was in the driveway, the engine clicking and ticking as it cooled down. He could imagine her opening up the powerful automobile on the coast road, as if the car were flesh and muscle instead of rubber and steel, running it like a racehorse through the tight turns and short straight-aways, downshifting and double clutching, the engine wailing with force as gas pumped into the cylinders like life-giving blood.

Night was coming down now and he could hear but not see the ever-pounding breakers on the beach below the house. A light came on in one of the upper windows and Cather-ine Tramell passed across the panes like a phantom. A moment later she returned to the window and looked out. He darted out of sight, sure he had been seen, but she was gazing out to the dark sea, hypnotized.

Languidly, she began to unbutton her blouse and slipped out of it and stood for a second or two bare-breasted, framed in the window. Then she drew the curtain, her image a languorous wisp on the material. Nick Curran stared intently at the window, the roaring of the surf in his ears, his eyes wide and intense.

Then the light went out and he thought of her sliding alone into her clean bed.

He was back in San Francisco within the hour, hunched over a computer terminal in the darkened, deserted detective room. His hands flew over the keyboard. He typed in: Hazel Dobkins, white female, 145 Albion Avenue, Mill Valley, then hit "enter" and waited for the big electronic brain to think it over.

First, the computer flew through the files of the SFPD memory and reported NKA— police shorthand for "Nothing Known Against."

"Shit," Nick breathed quietly, though he wasn't really surprised. Hazel Dobkins looked like your typical cat-loving, pie-baking grandmother. The chance of her having a parking ticket was slim, never mind a history of priors.

The machine waited expectantly for Nick's command. "What the hell," he said aloud and punched in the archive code for crimes committed in the state of California, from Ukiah all the way down to Baja; he reentered Hazel Dobkins's ID, waited and got what he expected. Instantly the computer came back with: Dobkins, Hazel, C: Nothing Current. Of course, "Nothing Current" isn't quite the same as "Clean."

The computer thought about it a little longer and then flashed more information on the screen. Nick felt a little charge of excitement as he read the data: Dobkins, Hazel, C: Released, San Quentin, July 7, 1965.

"Hiya, Hazel," he whispered. Swiftly, he typed in the codes that would pull up her prior arrest record and was rewarded instantly: Indict 4 counts, homicide, July 1955—Trial, January 10–11, 1956—GAC— San Francisco Superior Court.

"Four counts," murmured Nick. He touched the GAC—Guilty As Charged—on the screen, as if reassuring himself that it was actually there.

"Ain't you got nothing better to do than come in here and jack ·off that damn machine?" said a voice behind him.

Curran never took his eyes off the screen. "What are you doing here, cowboy?"

Gus Moran dropped into a chair next to Nick Curran. "I came in here to jack off the damn machine, sonny. Same as you." He punched his partner lightly in the shoulder. "Great minds, huh, Nicky?"

Curran managed to tear his eyes from the screen. "What did you find out over in Berkeley, Gus?"

"I made the acquaintance of various law enforcement professionals and I eyeballed the coeds. There are some fine-looking girls over there, Nick."

"Forget it, Gus. They're all too smart for you."

"Yeah, well, there's a lot a seasoned older man could teach them, you know."

"What did *you* learn?"

"I learned all about one dead professor of psychology. Noah Goldstein. *Doctor* Noah Goldstein. Dead of multiple stab wounds, September 1977. And guess what?"

"What? She did it?"

"Can't prove that, sonny, but they knew each other. Doctor Noah Goldstein was academic counselor to young Catherine Tramell."

"Was she ever a suspect?"

"Nope. No, sir. They never even got a statement from Miss Catherine Tramell. They had no suspects. No one had anything against Doctor Goldstein. No arrests. No nothing. The case is still open—but good luck after all these years. That is one cold trail, partner."

"Not if it could be linked to the Boz killing."

He craned his neck and peered at the information on Nick's computer screen. "Jesus Christ! Hazel Dobkins! Talk about cold trails." He looked pityingly at Nick, shaking his head. "Thanks a lot, sonny. I haven't thought of old Hazel in years."

"You know her?"

Gus snorted. "Know her? Couldn't get it outta my head for years. Nice little housewife—three little kids—nice husband who wasn't porkin' around, no financial problems. No history of mental illness, nothing."

"And?"

"And, one day little Hazel gets up, and out of the clear blue sky she takes it into her head to do 'em all. *All* of 'em. Used a—"

"An ice pick?" said Nick hopefully.

"Simmer down, sonny. She used a carving knife. Got it as a wedding present. First she did her husband. Carved him up like a Thanksgiving turkey. Then she did her

three kids. Place looked like a slaughter-
house by the time she was finished."

"Jesus," breathed Nick.

"Jesus didn't have a whole lot to do with
it, Nicky. When Hazel was done wiping out
her whole family, she calls the police and
that's where they find her, sitting in her living room, knife in her lap. No denial, no
insanity, no nothing."

"But why? Why did she do it?"

Gus Moran shrugged. "That was the amazing thing, Nick. No one knows. Headshrink-
ers couldn't explain it. And God knows,
Hazel couldn't figure it out. Said she didn't
know why she done it."

"Unbelievable."

"If you didn't know, how come you were
sitting here taking a stroll down memory
lane with Hazel?"

Quickly, Nick explained his tail of Catherine Tramell that day and of her involve-
ment with Hazel Dobkins.

"Jeez," said Gus Moran, "nice friends
she's got."

CHAPTER NINE

He got back to the beach house just after noon the next day. Catherine Tramell answered the door, wearing a tight-fitting little black dress. The fabric fit like a jet-black second skin, setting off her golden hair and deep blue eyes.

"Hi," she said simply.

"Am I disturbing you?"

"No."

"Stupid question, I guess. Nothing ever disturbs you, does it?"

"Why don't you come in?" She opened the door wide and walked away, leading the way into the house. Nick Curran followed, his eyes watching her taut, firm buttocks moving under her dress.

Things were much the same in the room as they had been the last time he had been there—except there were more clippings on the table, a full newspaper history of the rocky career of Detective Nick Curran, SFPD. She picked up one of the clippings and looked at it then showed it to him.

KILLER COP TO FACE POLICE REVIEW blared the headline.

"I'm using you for my detective."

"*Your* detective?"

"My detective. In my book. I hope you don't mind. You *don't* mind, do you?"

"Would it make a difference if I did mind?"

She smiled and slipped away from the question like a fighter dodging a couple of jabs. "Would you like a drink? I was just going to have one."

"No, thanks."

She nodded to herself. "That's right, I forgot. You've abandoned all your old vices. No scotch, no Jack Daniel's. No cigarettes, no drugs." She smiled over her shoulder. "No sex?"

Catherine didn't wait for an answer. She went to the bar, a crowd of bottles gathered on a marble slab, and a block of ice set in a shallow sink.

"I want to ask you a few questions," Nick said quietly.

There was an ice pick in her hands and she started chipping away at the block. "I wanted to ask you some too."

"You did?"

The ice crackled and shattered as she struck again and again at the ice. "Questions for my book."

"You got something against ice cubes?"

"I like rough edges."

She was giving the ice a real working over,

splintering it into fragments. She raised her arm and plunged it over and over again into the block, putting force behind each blow.

"What did you want to ask me?" he asked.

She was finished with the ice now. She tossed aside the ice pick and scooped a handful of shards into her glass and filled it with Jack Daniel's.

"Tell me, Nick, how does it feel to kill someone?" She asked in the same tone of voice that one home owner might say another: Just what do *you* do to get rid of your crabgrass?

"How does it feel? Why don't you tell me?"

"I don't know. But *you* do. How do you feel? Powerful? Sorrowful? Sick? Elated? A mixture of all four? Or is it something else? Something you just can't know until you've actually taken a life?"

Disgust—for her, for his brutal past—flashed across his face. "It was an accident. They got in the line of fire. Killing is never . . . It was an accident, that's all."

"How does an accident like that happen, Nick? Do they just happen? Didn't you just itch to pull that trigger?"

"It was an accident," Nick insisted hotly. "I was undercover. I was on a drug buy. It happens."

"Just happens?"

"Yeah. You don't plan anything. No killing like that, on a drug buy, is planned in advance. Not like—"

"Johnny?"

"I was going to say Professor Goldstein. Noah Goldstein. You know the name?"

"It's a name from the past, Nick. Fourteen years in the past."

"You want a name from the present? How does the name Hazel Dobkins strike you?"

Without taking her eyes from his face, she took a sip from her drink. Her skin was so luminously white he imagined, for a moment, that he could see the brown liquid sliding down her smooth throat.

"Dobkins? Goldstein? Where should I start?"

"Let's start with Goldstein."

"Noah was my counselor my freshman year." She smiled. "You know, that's probably where I got the idea for the ice pick. For my book. Funny how the subconscious works, isn't it?"

"Hilarious."

"I should have said peculiar how the subconscious works, shouldn't I have?"

"Hazel Dobkins? What about her?"

She hesitated a moment. "Hazel is my friend," she said finally.

Nick Curran recalled Gus's words of the night before: *Jeez, nice friends she's got.* "Your friend? Your friend wiped out her whole family. Three kids!"

"She was arrested, tried and she went to jail. She hasn't been in trouble once in the last thirty-five years. Like they say, Nick, she was rehabilitated. Though I'll bet cops prefer: She paid her debt to society."

"I don't give a damn one way or the other. What I want to know is why? Why is she your friend? Or do you just collect freaks?"

"She wiped out her whole family. She's helped me understand the homicidal impulse."

"But *she* doesn't understand why she did it."

"Sounds to me like you just don't approve of my choice of friends, Nick."

"Sounds to me like you could have learned a lot more about the 'homicidal impulse' in school. You must have studied that at Berkeley."

"Only the theory." She sipped her drink and watched him over the top of her glass. "Course, you know all about the homicidal impulse, don't you? Not the theory, the practice. You know all about it, don't you . . . Shooter?"

"Shooter?"

"What happened, Nick?" she asked softly. "Did you get sucked into it? Did you *like* it?"

"No one ever likes it. No one in their right mind."

"And you? Were you in your right mind? Tell me about the coke, Nick. The day you shot those two tourists—how much coke did you do that day? Or the night before? What was your habit, Nick? A quarter of a gram?

Half? Or did you do a whole unit? Pretty tough guy."

The softer her voice, the more barbed her words seemed to become.

"I don't know what the hell you're talking about. I doubt that you do. You're just a rich girl playing games. You said you like games, didn't you?"

She was closer to him now. She had put down her drink. "You can tell me, Nick. Were you stoned, Nick? So wired that the idea of blowing away a couple of citizens kind of appealed to you? Or were you just having coming-down jitters and your hand was shaky? *That* would make it an accident. An accident that might have sent you to jail, definitely would have gotten you thrown off the force. But it would have been an accident. Nothing you could blame yourself for. A mistake. An accident."

"I was cleared," he protested. "There wasn't even a civil suit. It *was* an accident. Drugs were involved but I was buying the blow, not using it. Got it?"

She put her soft hand to his cheek and stroked, as she might a cat. "You can tell me, Nick," she said, her voice satiny smooth, seductive.

He grabbed her hand roughly. "I did not do drugs."

"Yes, you did." She was close now, he could feel her breath on his face, smell it. It was sweet, like her perfume. "They never tested you, did they? But Internal Affairs knew. They knew all along."

"If IA had known anything they would have—"

"Your wife knew, didn't she?" Her voice was velvety. "She knew what was going on. Nicky got too close to the flame. Nicky liked it, didn't he?"

Nick broke. He yanked her arm hard and twisted it behind her, pain shooting up her arm. Then he pulled her close. She was unfazed. Their eyes blazed, burrowing into each other's brains.

"Nicky liked it." whispered Catherine Tramell. "And Nicky's wife couldn't take it. That's why she killed herself."

The temperature in the room changed. The breakers were louder. The front door had opened and Roxy stood there. Her hair was tied up tight on the top of her lovely head and she was dressed from head to toe in black: a black leather motorcycle jacket over a black T-shirt; black jeans thrust into black boots. She shot a black look at Nick.

Catherine Tramell broke free of Nick. "Hiya, hon," she said brightly, like a housewife welcoming hubby home from the office. She went to Roxy and kissed her lightly on the lips. It could have been simply a chic, Euro-trash style greeting. It could have meant more. She draped her arm across Roxy's slender shoulders. "You two have met, haven't you?"

Nick didn't have to hear any more. There was a red-hot anger building in his brain and, from the hazy clouds of brutal murder, casual sin, and intense attraction, one thing was becoming clear: Catherine Tramell might have been an extraordinary woman, but she was not a seer. She couldn't know all she knew from simple deduction. It took more than a BA in psychology from Berkeley to make you omniscient. Nick knew he had been sold out.

He pushed by Roxy and Catherine, fury burning within him, white and hot like a magnesium flare.

"You're not leaving are you, Nick?" asked Catherine, her lovely face the picture of innocence. "It's early yet."

"Let him go, sugar," said Roxy.

Nick betrayed nothing, his face was as set and as hard as an ancient mask. He went through the doorway without a backward glance.

"You're going to make a terrific character, Nick," Catherine called after him.

He didn't care. Right then, he was more interested in fact than fiction.

CHAPTER TEN

Nick Curran probably set some kind of record for traveling between Stinson Beach and downtown San Francisco. As he blew along the highway, a single thought burned through his mind: He had been sold out, sold out to Catherine Tramell. He didn't know why, but he had a good idea how.

Cops use informers every day. In fact, rare is the case that isn't broken by information purchased or extorted from a snitch. Cops like Nick ran a dozen stoolies, snitches in the drug world, the mob, the Vietnamese gangs, the Jamaican posses, and the Chinese tongs. The easy betrayal of confidences is the bedrock of police work; criminals hate squealers and so do cops, oddly enough. Perhaps it's the recognition of the similarities between the outlaw life and law enforcement—they are both brotherhoods with their own codes, credos, and taboos—that makes for this small patch of common ground. Despite their reliance on them, cops are steeped in disdain and contempt for snitches. So it was particularly galling to Nick to think that someone had informed on him.

He burst out of the elevator on the tenth floor of police headquarters and charged down the hall to Beth Garner's office. Her secretary stopped typing for a split second and tried to stop him from barging into Beth's office.

"She's on the phone. She'll be right with you, Detective Curran. I'll tell her you're here."

"Never mind," barked Nick. "I'll just drop in." He almost kicked in the door. He was enraged, angry enough to kill someone.

Curran grabbed the phone out of Beth Garner's hand and slammed it down in the cradle. He leaned over her desk until his face was close to hers. She remembered their last meeting and shrank from him in dread.

"Who has access to my file?"

Beth Garner paled. "What are you talking about, Nick? What's come over you? What's wrong?"

Nick's words were clear and clipped, and steel-tipped with hostility. "Who has got access to my goddamn file?"

"Nick—"

Curran seized her by her thin shoulders and pulled her roughly out of her chair. "Don't get innocent with me. Don't give me any bullshit about doctor-patient confidentiality. I'm going to ask you again, and I want an answer: Who did you give my file to?"

He didn't have to threaten. She knew far too well that he was capable of violence. "Nobody," she said. She was unable to look him in the eye.

"I'm warning you, Beth."

"It's a confidential psychiatric record, Nick. It would be illegal to—"

"That's the bullshit I said I didn't want to hear, Beth."

"But it's *true*."

He shook his head. "No it isn't. Don't, Beth. Don't lie to me."

"Nick, I—"

"It's Internal Affairs, isn't it?" he said suddenly. "IA got to you and gave you some crap that you fell for hook, line, and sinker. Right?"

"Nick, they told me that—"

"Who?" demanded Nick. "Who's 'they,' Beth?"

She swallowed hard. "Nilsen," she blurted.

"That's all I wanted to hear, Beth."

Nick Curran blew into the Internal Affairs Division office a minute later, exploding like a grenade. He strode down the line of desks heading straight for Nilsen with the accuracy of a laser-guided missile. The fat detective was sitting, leaning back in his padded chair, his eyes on that afternoon's *Examiner*, a cup of coffee coming up to his lips.

With one backhand blow, Nick swatted the paper and the cup out of Nilsen's pudgy hand, coffee slopping over his messy desk and rumpled suit.

"Jesus Christ, Curran!" Nilsen vaulted out of his chair, his face red with anger. "What the fuck—"

Nick was on him. He picked him up by the lapels and slammed him against the wall. Curran was right on the edge, a hair's breadth from losing control. "You sold her my file, didn't you, you sonofabitch!"

Nilsen looked into Curran's eyes and saw blind rage. Fear pulsed through him. "What are you talking about? Are you out of your fuckin'—"

Nick body-slammed Nilsen again, the cop's head smacking against the wall. The other officers in the room had been paralyzed for a moment but were now rushing to their brother's rescue.

"What did she pay you, you slimy motherfucker?"

One of the Internal Affairs investigators grabbed Nick by the shoulder and tried to pull him off Nilsen. Nick thrust him away as if he were no stronger than a child. He got a death grip on Nilsen's jowly throat and squeezed. "*What did she pay you?*"

Nilsen couldn't have answered, even if he wanted to. Nick's strong hand had closed his windpipe and the detective's eyes were bugging out. His face turned scarlet.

"Curran!" yelled one of the cops in the room. "For Christ's sake, you're gonna kill him."

Nick didn't care. His clutch tightened. He was blind to everything except the fearful, florid face in front of him and he felt the smooth and calming desire to kill flood through him. The room, the other men in it were far away. All that mattered to Nick was hatred.

Then, abruptly, he was wrenched back to reality by the cold, deadly, unmistakably weighty presence of a gun barrel laid gently behind his right ear.

"Let him go," said one of the shooflies calmly. "Let him go, Curran. Nice and easy."

Nick froze, but his grip eased just enough for Nilsen to draw a single tortured breath. Curran looked over his shoulder. He loosed his grip completely and Nilsen doubled over, hacking and gagging, scrabbling at his bruised throat.

The cop with the gun at Nick's head spoke again, still calmly. "Now if you and Nilsen have a little difference of opinion I suggest you settle it outside the office. Okay? Now, Curran, you just walk out of here. Not another word. No funny stuff. Just turn and walk. Got it?"

"Got it," said Nick soberly.

"That's good. Now go."

Nick Curran turned and started to walk calmly from the room, ignoring the blunt snouts of the pistols still trained on him.

Nilsen, however, was not so calm. He had hauled himself upright, his face still crimson with pain, hurt pride, and rage.

"You fucked yourself, Shooter!" he screamed at Nick's back. "Do you hear me? You're out! You are out of this department if it's the last thing I do! *You're out!*"

Nick did not seem to hear the enraged cop; or, if he did, care.

It didn't take long for news of the blowup between Nick Curran and Nilsen to spread through headquarters. Cops like gossip just as much as anyone else. Gus Moran was alarmed when he heard what had happened. It was one thing to get into feuds with other policemen—even higher ups like Talcott—it was another thing altogether to get Internal Affairs pissed off at you. The guys in IA could make your life unbearable if they chose to. It was their job to hound cops off the force. Nick was already skating on thin ice with the shooflies. Now he was sure to fall through and into the frigid waters of a section investigation.

Gus caught up with Nick as he stormed out of the building and into the police parking lot. There was no doubt in Moran's mind where a *normal* cop would be headed after a bust-up with a guy from Internal Affairs— the nearest bar, but not the Ten-Four. But with a mad dog like Curran, there was no telling where he was going or what kind of trouble he would land himself in.

"Nick! Nick! Wait up!" By the time he got to his partner Gus was wheezing and puffing, the legacy of too many cigarettes and too much beer. "What the hell is goin' down, son? It's all over the building you tried to kill Nilsen. With your bare hands, yet. You're gonna have to control that temper, sonny, or you are gonna land in hot water."

Nick took a deep breath. He couldn't be angry at Gus Moran. He was the only person on the force who really gave a damn about him. "Look, don't worry about it. Nothing's going to happen. I'll be okay."

Ruefully, Gus Moran shook his head. "No, sir. No, you won't be okay. You know it, I know it. They're gonna want your badge."

"Maybe they can have it."

"Nicky, you don't mean that."

Curran's shoulders slumped as fatigue and despair washed over him. "I don't know what I mean. All I know for sure is that I'm sick and tired of being played with."

Gus could only smile that crooked smile of his. "And you know what? From what I hear, you have a real conclusive way of demonstrating that."

"She knows, Gus."

There was no need to identify "she." They both knew that Catherine Tramell was bad news.

"Knows? Knows what? She's only fuckin' with your head, sonny. Forget about it."

"She knows where I live, she knows how I live. She's inside my head. She's coming after me and I'm gonna be ready for her."

"What is it between you two?"

For a moment, Nick Curran wrestled with his fears and desires and his brooding fasci nation with Catherine Tramell. Long before he realized it, she was under his skin, gnaw- ing at something deep inside his soul. He shook his head and almost smiled. "I don't know. I just don't know what the hell is going on."

"But something, *something*'s goin' on."

"Yeah. Something."

Gus Moran wrapped a fleshy arm around his partner's shoulders. "The hell with it, I'll take a vacation day. Lemme buy you a drink."

"Naw, I don't think so. I've got to go some- where and think."

"Just don't go to Stinson to do your think- ing, Nick."

"No, don't worry. I won't." Nick started to walk away.

"Hey, sonny, do me a favor."

Nick stopped and half turned toward his partner. "Anything for you, Gus."

"Just be careful."

Nick Curran smiled. "Well, *almost* any- thing. But not that."

Moran shrugged. "Yeah. That's kinda what I figured. You know, Nick, something is happening to you I never guessed woulda happened."

"Really? What's that?"

Gus Moran smiled broadly. "Your wackiness. It's becoming predictable."

The laugh track screamed in hysterical laughter, convulsions of hilarity about something or other spraying out of Nick's TV. He sat in a chair in front of the set peering intently at the lame sit-com on the screen. He had a bottle of Jack Daniel's cradled in his lap like a baby and a cigarette dangled from his lips. The ashtray at his elbow was full to overflowing; the bottle was half empty.

Nick looked as if he was watching the show, studying it hard, as if it were a difficult foreign film with subtitles and not some moronic half hour of network high-jinks. The truth was that he wasn't seeing the show at all. He couldn't tell you what had set off the paroxysms of canned laughter. He didn't even know the name of the show—so deep was he in thought.

Like a debilitating poison, Catherine Tramell had infused herself in his blood, spreading to every part of his being. His bewilderment, his disorientation was like a fever; he saw, with crystal clarity, but with a fantastic air of unreality, a whole range of tableaux. He could see himself making love to her, passionately, tenderly. He could see himself killing her, coldheartedly blowing her away with his .38. He could see himself doing both. . . .

He had no idea how long someone had been knocking at the door and he scarcely moved a muscle when he heard Beth Garner's worried voice, calling to him through the door. "Nick. Nick, I know you're there. Please open the door."

His eyes flicked to the door, as if he could see through it to her. "Go away, Beth. I'm watching my favorite TV show."

Her voice was beseeching. "Nick, please."

"I don't want to see you," he said curtly.

There was a moment of silence and he thought that she had simply gone away. Then came the sound of a key turning in the lock, the dead bolt sliding back. The door swung open and Beth stood in the doorway, tentative and afraid.

"I still have my key," she said. She held up the key, displaying it as if he might not believe her.

Nick Curran sucked the last drag out of the cigarette butt in his mouth, inhaling till the cigarette burnt down to the filter, singeing his knuckles. "I said, I don't want you here, Beth." He reached for another cigarette and lit it. "Just put the key on the table and leave."

Even Beth Garner had a temper. She threw the key ring to the floor at his feet. "Damn it, Nick, don't shut me out! You owe me more than that."

Calmly, he stood, carefully put down his

bottle and retrieved the key ring. "I don't owe you anything, Beth. You don't owe me anything either. We went to bed—what was it?—ten or fifteen times."

"I wasn't aware you were keeping score," she said evenly.

"Don't flatter yourself, Beth. It was never memorable enough to carry any obligations."

Her eyes narrowed, flashing loathing like a torch. "Sometimes I really hate you."

Nick smiled, but there was no amusement in his eyes. "Yeah? Well, why don't you find yourself a friendly therapist and work out some of that hostility." He paused a moment to draw on his cigarette. "See, if you work out some of *your* problems, Beth, then you'll be sparing yourself a tragedy."

"Tragedy? What the hell are you talking about?"

"Maybe you'll be able to get off once in a while—before the next guy dies of boredom."

Beth flinched as if she had been slapped. His venomous, vile words hung in the air between them for a moment, then they fell like gasoline on a fire.

Beth's lips curled and she threw herself at him, her hands curled into claws, her red nails like talons. He could feel the heat of her anger radiating like lava. She wanted to scratch his eyes out. She wanted to taste his blood on her lips. She wanted to hurt him more than he had ever been hurt before.

Nick caught her by the wrists and held her at bay, feeling her abhorrence of him throbbing in her veins, pulsating in her muscles and sinews. She writhed for an instant, her anger blazing, then burning so hot it burnt itself out. As quickly as it erupted, it was spent and she went limp in his arms. He pushed her away.

Beth Garner buried her face in her hands for a moment and trembled as she took stock of the animosity she had felt only a split second before. No one is more aware of the dangers of losing control than a trained therapist.

"I'm sorry," she whispered. "I'm sorry. I don't usually act like that."

Nick Curran looked at her with something approaching pity. He shook his head slowly. "How could you have let him, Beth? How could you give that scum my file? I trusted you, Beth. You might not believe it, but I did."

"I'm sorry, Nick. But I had to. I had to give him the file. I couldn't see any other way."

"Had to? Any other way? For what, for God's sake? You had to know that giving Nilsen my—" He waved her off. "Forget it. It doesn't matter anymore."

Tears were pooling in the corners of Beth Garner's wide brown eyes. "Nick, he was going to recommend your discharge from the force. He didn't buy my evaluation. Said I wasn't objective. So I made a deal with him to review the session notes for himself. I

didn't think he'd show them to anybody."
She looked at him imploringly.

For a moment, he was tempted to take her
in his arms and comfort her, but then a cold
wave of disdain washed over him. His face
turned to stone. "You did it for me?"

"Yes, yes, that's right. I care about you. I
did it for you."

"Didn't you see? Objective! That's a good
one. When it comes to me and Nilsen, Sig-
mund Freud himself couldn't be objective
enough for that bastard. He wanted dirt on
me, Beth, and you were the best source. He
tricked you into selling me out. He tricked
you and you fell for it."

"Nick, please—"

He turned his back on her. "Get out of
here, Beth," he said softly. "Please."

"I wish you'd—"

"Go, Beth." He picked up his Jack Daniel's bottle, took a long swig

She looked beseechingly at him for a
moment longer, but she knew in her heart
that she had lost him, that betrayal was the
one sin he would never forgive.

Hours later, deep in the night, the Jack
Daniel's long gone, the TV broadcast dis-
solved into a fuzzy cloud of static, Nick
Curran slept fitfully on his couch. His
alcohol-addled brain was filled by a miasma
of disordered dreams, dead bodies, desperate drinks, and spent bullets. There was a
tangle of images: Catherine Tramell, Roxy,

Gus, Beth, Talcott, and Walker. There were
the deformed and distorted pictures that
Catherine hung in her living room; Johnny
Boz's punctured body oozing blood. These
melded with purely imagined images—
Hazel Dobkins killing her children and her
husband all those years ago.

Somewhere in his brain he knew that he
had to stop all the killing. He had to sound
the alarm. Then, miraculously, the bells
started ringing.

He awoke with a start to the shrill pealing
of the telephone.

CHAPTER ELEVEN

He lunged for the phone as if it were a life-line. The words he heard cut through the haze in his brain as if they were poisoned darts. Nick felt the pool of bourbon in his stomach slosh like the bilges on an old boat.

"Yeah," he managed to say, "okay."

He couldn't put a name to the voice on the other end of the telephone line, but he knew the instant he heard it that he was listening to a cop and the cop was talking officially. The policeman rapped out a few terse sentences. He told Nick what had happened and where he was expected inside of five minutes, then hung up.

Curran had woken up drunk, but the effect of the message dissipated his intoxication faster than a summer sun burns off a morning mist. Sober though he was now, the shock of what he had heard kept him locked in place on the couch. A few moments passed before he had the strength to haul himself upright and out the door.

*   *   *

He found the usual crime-scene carnival in the parking lot behind the Ten-Four. Maybe this one was a little bigger, considering a cop was involved, with police cruisers everywhere and uniforms standing around as if they expected the criminal to return to the scene of the crime. It struck Nick, as he got out of his Mustang, that they might be looking at him in just that light.

Walker, Gus, and a couple of the guys from Internal Affairs were standing around a big, gold, Lincoln Town Car. None of them looked happy to see Nick—not that he was ecstatic about seeing them, if it came to that. The crowd around the car parted as Nick approached, as if he carried the plague.

Gus Moran shone a flashlight on the wide front seat of the luxurious car. Martin Nilsen, late of the Internal Affairs Division, San Francisco Police Department, sprawled there. Dark, almost black blood puddled on the velour headrest in a grim halo around his head.

"One shot," muttered Gus. "Fired at close range. Looks like a .38 caliber revolver."

None of the men there had to be told that a .38 was the standard-issue firearm of the SFPD.

"Give me your gun, Nick," Walker said almost apologetically.

"Jesus Christ, Phil," said Nick quietly, "you can't believe that I—"

"Just give me your gun, Nick. Please."

Curran shrugged, slipped the weapon out of his shoulder holster and handed it over. The chief of Homicide took it and sniffed the barrel, like a wine connoisseur testing a wine of dubious vintage and then shook his head. He passed the gun to one of the Internal Affairs men.

"Well, it's not much, Nick, but this gun hasn't been fired recently."

"Not since I checked out on the police range two, maybe three weeks ago. I didn't kill Nilsen. You know that."

"All I know is that he didn't get killed with that gun, Nick. That's all I can say for sure." Walker didn't look Nick in the eye. He just turned and stalked away heading for his own car.

Curran looked from face to face and at Walker's retreating back. "You think *I* . . ."

"I don't, son," said Gus, "But I gotta tell you, I got the feeling that I'm the minority opinion around here."

Lieutenant Jake Sullivan, also of Internal Affairs and almost the pain in the ass that Nilsen had been, stepped forward with an "I'm in charge here" look on his face.

"Curran, you get down to headquarters now. We should have a little talk." Sullivan didn't sound like he was inviting Curran for a friendly chat over a cup of coffee.

"Am I a suspect, Sullivan?"

"Maybe."

"Then read me my rights and book me."

It struck Nick that he spoke almost the same words that Catherine Tramell had used on him.

Sullivan shrugged. "You want to do it that way, Curran, we can oblige you."

"It would be a pleasure," said Morgan, another hard-ass from IA.

"C'mon, Nick," said Gus Moran, getting between his partner and the two cops. "Do yourself a favor for once in your life. Just cooperate with these guys."

For a moment, it looked as if Curran would demand his constitutionally guaranteed right to be Miranda-ized and cuffed, but there was no greater humiliation for a cop and even he was not up to it. "I'll go downtown, Sullivan, just to prove to you that I always cooperate with law enforcement like a good, upstanding citizen."

"Good."

"And to prove to you that I didn't kill this—" He nodded toward Nilsen's corpse. "This police officer."

"Nothing would please me more, Curran," said Sullivan, but no one believed he meant it.

They took Nick to the same interrogation room they had used when questioning Catherine Tramell. Walker, Talcott, and Gus Moran sat in, but away from the table, in the background, while Sullivan and Morgan took center stage giving Nick Curran the third degree. Everybody knew this was

Internal Affair's show and that IA would nail Nick or give him a clean bill of health.

"You didn't like Marty Nilsen, did you, Curran?" said Morgan, as if scoring some kind of showy forensic coup in a hotly contested debate.

"That was common knowledge. I'll bet there're people you don't like, Morgan. I'll bet there are a lot of people who don't like you."

"That ain't the point."

"You attacked him this afternoon," said Sullivan, "in plain view of a dozen police officers."

"That's right. So what? Okay. So I went after him. I lost my temper."

"Maybe you never found your temper. Maybe you waited for Marty outside the Ten-Four and put a slug in his head. Maybe you wanted to get back at him for riding you so hard. It's possible, right?"

"I didn't give a shit about Nilsen riding me, Morgan. I hardly noticed him."

"Then what got under your skin?" asked Sullivan. "How come you hated him so much?"

"I didn't hate him. But he ... Listen, Nilsen got hold of my psychiatric file. The one the department compiled right after I wasted those tourists."

Talcott winced. He hated to hear something so horrible put so bluntly. He would have much preferred Beth Garner's clinical terms—trauma or incident.

"That's bullshit!" said Morgan hotly.

"I know he did. But more than that, he was using it. He was showing it outside the department. He was using my own file against me."

"Do you have any proof of that? Do you have any evidence that he actually showed your psychiatric file to anyone? Do you even have any proof that he *had* your file?"

Of course, Nick did. He had a lot of proof. But if he told them about Catherine Tramell and her uncanny insights into his mind and manner, they would think he had completely flipped. If he told them that Beth Garner had confessed to giving the file to Nilsen, then she would get in trouble. There was only one thing he could do: lie.

"I'm asking for proof, Curran. Do you have any?"

Nick Curran shook his head. "No. No, I don't have any proof of anything."

"Then you got nothing," observed Morgan.

"Except that I'm not crazy enough to mix it up with someone, then a couple of hours later blow them away with a service .38. That's got to count for something, right?"

"Not much. People do crazy things sometimes. You know that, Curran."

The door to the interrogation room opened and Beth Garner came in. There were dark circles under her eyes, as if she had been awake all night, not just pulled from her bed by bad news. She glanced with worried eyes at Nick Curran.

"And here's our expert on people doing crazy things now," said Morgan.

The last person Sullivan wanted on the scene was Curran's own personal head-shrinker. "We'll speak to you afterwards if you don't mind, Doctor Garner."

"I'd like to sit in, I think I could help."

"I'd really rather—"

Oddly enough, it was Talcott who broke the stalemate. It would look better to have Nick Curran branded a crazy cop than to have to admit to the outside world that a member of the San Francisco Police Department had killed a brother officer in cold blood.

"I don't see anything wrong with Doctor Garner sitting in, if Detective Curran doesn't object."

Nick shrugged. "I don't care."

Beth Garner nodded and took a chair, sitting forward in it, anxious and tense.

"Where were you tonight?" demanded Morgan.

"Home," said Nick. "I was watching TV."

"All night?"

"Yeah."

"What were you watching?"

"I don't know. Some bullshit." He could hardly recall having the television set on, never mind the programs that were on the screen.

"Were you drinking?" asked Sullivan.

Curran's eyes flicked over to Beth like high beams. "Yeah. I was drinking."

Sullivan frowned. "I thought you were not supposed to be drinking."

"I wasn't drinking for a long time. Couple of months I was dry as a bone. Now, when I go home I have a couple of drinks. I can handle it. And I don't drink when I'm not supposed to. I don't drink on duty, just like a good cop."

"But you *were* drinking?"

"Just said I was."

"How much?"

"Couple of drinks. Like I said."

"When did you start again? You were dry for so long."

"I started a couple of days ago. I stopped drinking because *I* wanted to. I started again because *I* wanted to. You have a problem with that, Lieutenant?"

"No, no problem. Just so long as you didn't get a bellyful and then decide to go out and do something stupid. That's all."

Beth Garner broke in. "I saw Detective Curran at his apartment around ten o'clock tonight. He was sober and lucid." She spoke in her best, detached clinician's voice.

Sullivan eyed her suspiciously. "And just what were you doing at Detective Curran's apartment last night at ten o'clock, if you don't mind my asking?"

Beth hesitated only a split second before replying. "I was there in my capacity as his departmental therapist. I had heard about his altercation with Lieutenant Nilsen and I thought he might need some counseling."

"In the middle of the night?" Morgan scoffed.

"It was not the middle of the night, Lieutenant. I told you, it was about ten o'clock. And whatever you might think of my profession, you should remember that I am on call, twenty-four hours a day."

"Very impressive," sneered Morgan. "Very dedicated. Very convenient."

"And how did Detective Curran appear to you, Doctor?" asked Sullivan.

"As I said, he was lucid and sober. He expressed regret over the incident with Lieutenant Nilsen and he displayed no hostility."

"How long were you there?"

She looked squarely at Nick Curran, holding his gaze. "I was there about fifteen minutes. I saw there was no reason for my concern and I left."

Nick looked away and fumbled for a cigarette, lighting it and sucking the smoke hungrily into his lungs.

"There's no smoking in this building," snapped Morgan.

Walker, Talcott, and Gus Moran knew *exactly* what Curran would say next.

"What are you going to do—charge me with smoking?"

"Listen, Curran—" Morgan said angrily, half rising from his chair.

Sullivan cut off Morgan's tirade. "I'll ask you once, Nick. For the record: did you kill him?"

Nick didn't falter. "No."

"Are you sure?" insisted Sullivan.

"Come on. I've said it already. I'm going to storm into his office in the afternoon in front of everybody and then that night I'm going to kill him? Call it dumb, crazy—whatever. I'm not dumb enough or crazy enough for that."

"Going after him before like that," said Morgan, "that gets you off the hook for killing him. It gives you an alibi."

"Like writing a book about killing a guy gets you off the hook for killing him," declared Walker. He exchanged glances and smirks with Moran and Curran.

"You know, Lieutenant, you might just have a good point there," said Nick.

Sullivan and Morgan recognized that they were being left out of the joke and they didn't like it. "I don't understand," said Sullivan. "What the hell are you talking about? What book?"

"Forget about it, Jake," said Walker. "It's nothing. A private joke, that's all."

"A joke? A fuckin' IA investigator gets blown away and you hot-shit homicide dicks are making *jokes*? What kind of bullshit is that?" Morgan had gone very red in the face.

Talcott didn't think much of the joke either. "None of this is funny," he announced sternly. He stood up. "You're on leave, Curran." He looked pointedly at Beth Garner. "On leave pending the outcome of a psychiatric investigation." He didn't have to pronounce the rest of the sentence, they all knew what he meant: flunk the psycho test and Curran would be off the force.

The interrogation was over for the time being. Talcott swept out of the room trailing Sullivan and Morgan in his wake. Walker left alone.

Gus Moran scratched the stubble on his cheek. "What do you say, Nick, Doc, let's go get some breakfast. Nice big plate of old-fashioned police grease: couple of eggs over easy, sausage, bacon. My treat."

"Thanks, Gus, but I'll pass.

"What about you, Doc?"

"I'm going to walk Beth to her car, Gus."

Moran shrugged. "Guess that means no, huh? Well, I guess I'll buy the *Chronicle* and go close my arteries all by my lonesome." He shambled off, his shoulders slumped with fatigue and the weight of his cares.

Nick Curran took Beth Garner by the arm and steered her toward the door. Even the headquarters of a big city police department slows down in the hour just before dawn. The corridors were empty of cops and criminals, their places taken by a few janitors and cleaners. The halls were silent save for the hum of the machines used to buff the marble floors.

Beth shot him a sidelong glance, as if unsure of his state of mind.

Nick Curran sensed her inquiry. "I just

wanted to say thank you." He spoke quietly, his voice soft and gentle.

"It's the least I could do, Nick, considering how much of a mess I got you into with those reports."

"You didn't have to give me an alibi. After what I've said and done, you could have hung me out to dry."

"Why would I want to do a thing like that?"

Nick smiled wryly. "Because I would have deserved it."

"Forget about it." She smiled warmly. "How do you know Catherine Tramell saw your file?"

"Simple. She knows stuff about me that I only told you."

Beth Garner shook her head, as if in disbelief. "She must really be something. From a clinical point of view, I mean."

"What was she like in school?"

"I hardly knew her. She gave me the creeps, though."

Nick held open the big glass doors of the headquarters building. "The creeps? Why?"

Beth shivered. It was hard to tell if it was from the cold or the memory. "I . . . I don't know why. It was a long time ago, I don't really remember."

They stopped at her car. "Nick, you have to get some rest. Promise me you will."

"I promise."

She kissed him quickly, softly on the cheek. "Good." She fumbled for the keys to her car, found them and opened the door. "Go home now, Nick. Sleep for a couple of hours. You'll feel a lot better."

But there was something he could do right then that would make him feel better. "Beth, I didn't mean what I said. About—"

She held up her hand to stop him. "Yes you did. I'm a big girl. I can handle it."

"Beth—"

"Go home, Nick."

He stood in the parking lot and waited until she had driven away. He didn't go home. He waited until she was out of sight, then went in search of Gus to share a plate of pure cholesterol and wait for things to start humming at headquarters.

At nine o'clock Nick figured that Andrews would be in the office.

Walker frowned at him from his office when Nick entered the Homicide room. The glare was eloquent. It said: What the hell are you doing here?

"Just came in to clean out my desk," he called out.

"You've got five minutes, Nick," Walker yelled back. "Then get the hell out of here."

"Hey, no problem." He hoped he looked the picture of aggrieved innocence. Andrews was sitting at his desk, typing furiously, making sense of the notes scribbled on the legal pad next to the typewriter.

"Hey, how you doing, Sam?"

Andrews looked at Nick with exaggerated

suspicion. "How am I doing? I'm doing fine, Nick. What about you? You're going to end up with the SFPD record for psycho leave taken."

"It's just a talent I've got," said Nick, ambling over to Andrews's desk. He glanced at Walker in his glass cubicle, then lowered his voice. "Did you find out about her parents?"

"You're on leave, man," whispered Andrews. "*Psycho* leave, Nick. I'm talking to a possible wacko here."

Nick grinned. "You know I'm a wacko, Sam. What did you find out?"

Andrews shot a look at Walker, then let his eyes drop to his report. "The boat blew. There was a leak in the gas line and a record of two previous repairs. There were two insurance policies on the Tramells, heavyweights, five million apiece. There was an investigation. Not just us, but the insurance company had PI's swarming all over the place. They didn't want to pay out ten million cash. But no one turned up anything. Zilch. Goose egg. The insurance company held its nose and paid. Your premiums and mine went up a couple of cents. It was an accident. That's official."

"And unofficially?"

Andrews shrugged. "What do you think?"

"So she got ten million bucks. So what? She already had a hundred million coming to her. She didn't do it for the insurance."
She did it for the thrill, he added mentally.

"Man, listen to me: as far as the world is concerned, she didn't do it at all. Remember that."

Nick nodded. "I'll try."

"Curran!"

"I'm on my way out, Phil," yelled Nick.

"Get in here before you go, Nick."

"Sure thing," he said affably. He strolled into Walker's office and shut the door. "What's on your mind, Phil?"

"I don't buy the Nick-Curran-Nice-Guy act, Nick. I know you too well."

"I'm just a soul whose intentions are good, Phil."

"Save it. Now listen. Internal Affairs is going to want to talk to you about Nilsen. They're handling the investigation. We're not. It's all theirs."

"The shooflies taking care of their own, huh? Correct me if I'm wrong, Phil, but a homicide is a homicide is a homicide, so where does IA get off conducting a murder investigation?"

"Now there's the Nick Curran I always knew." Walker shook his head. "I'm not going to argue this with you, Nick. It's none of my business and it's even less yours. Just follow these simple instructions: Make yourself available to IA when they want you. Stay out of trouble and stay in touch with Beth Garner. It'll help on the evaluation."

Nick folded his arms across his chest. "She killed him," he said bluntly.

"Jesus! You really are crazy! Now you've got Beth killing people."

"Don't be an asshole, Phil, I'm not talking about Beth, I'm talking about Catherine Tramell. She killed Nilsen."

"Really?"

"Yeah, really. She killed him. It's part of her game."

"Her game? First you've got her buying your file. Now you've got her killing Nilsen. Do me a favor, do yourself a favor, forget her, will you? Go someplace. Sit in the sun. Get her out of your system."

"You don't buy it do you? She *knew* nobody would buy it." He smiled and nodded, as if to himself. "You really have to admire her, you know. She figured all this out in advance, just like one of her damn books. She plotted this whole thing. She *knew* I'd say she did it. And she *knew* nobody would buy it."

Walker looked at him with something like pity. "She's screwing with your head Nick. Stay away from her."

"Hey," said Nick lightly, "no problem. I'm on vacation, right? Haven't got a care in the world."

CHAPTER TWELVE

Nick stayed out of trouble for almost fifteen minutes—the time it took for him to buck rush hour traffic between police headquarters and his apartment. Trouble, in the form of Catherine Tramell, was sitting on the front step of his building, her black Lotus parked at the curb.

"I heard about what happened," she said with a smile that stopped just short of being derisive. "What good is a shooter without his gun?"

Nick was in no mood to be teased. He was rarely in a mood to be teased. "How exactly did you hear?"

"I have attorneys. They have friends. I have friends. Money buys you a lot of attorneys and friends."

"I don't know about things like that. I don't have any money. I don't have any attorneys. And Gus is my only real friend."

She shrugged. "I wasn't talking about *real* friends. Why doesn't Gus like me?"

Nick Curran laughed. "Gus. Gus doesn't like you because he thinks you're bad for me. He's probably right. *I* like you. I like things that are bad for me."

"*Do* you?"

"Yeah. Do you want to come up for a drink?"

She glanced at the watch on her wrist, a slim delicate slip of platinum. "At nine in the morning? A little early, don't you think?"

"I've been up so long it's almost lunchtime as far as my body clock is concerned. Are you coming or not?"

She flashed him her most dazzling smile. "I thought you'd never ask me."

"I guess you don't know your character as well as you thought you did."

They started into the building, climbing the dark, shabby stairs to his third-floor apartment. She went ahead of him, talking over her shoulder.

"I'm learning," she said. "I'm learning all about you. Pretty soon I'll know you better than your friends do. Better than you know yourself."

"I told you, Gus is my only friend and he knows me better than he wants too, I bet. Don't be so sure of your own powers of analysis, either. You'll never figure me out completely."

"You don't think so? Why not?"

They stopped in front of the battered front door of his apartment and he dug in his pockets for his keys. "You'll never figure me out," he said, "because I'm very—"

In perfect synch, Catherine and Nick said the same word: "Unpredictable."

Nick tried not to frown and Catherine tried not to laugh at his predictability. He unlocked the door and ushered her into the apartment.

She was silent for a minute or two, standing in the center of the big, loftlike living room, examining the bare walls, the few pieces of furniture, the absence of personal touches that marked a space as specifically a home. The room was as impersonal as a hotel room.

"You should put some warmth into the place," she said at last.

"I'm not a warm person," he said curtly.

"I know. The room reflects your personality too graphically. I would have thought you'd want to hide that."

"I'm not trying to fool anybody," he called from the kitchenette, an alcove just inside the front door. He stood in the arch of the kitchen holding a full bottle of Jack Daniel's, the black seal unbroken.

"Jack Daniel's okay? It'll have to be. There isn't anything else."

"Fine."

"Ice?"

From the freezer compartment of the refrigerator, he took a block of ice, dumping it in the sink. From a drawer he took an ice pick, the shaft identical to the weapon used to dispatch Johnny Boz.

She looked at him, her eyebrows raised, silent question marks.

"I've been expecting you." He held up the ice pick, displaying it as if it were a trophy. "K mart. A dollar sixty-five."

It was a challenge and she accepted it. She took the ice pick and weighed it in her hand like a connoisseur. "Let me do the ice," she said coolly. "You like to watch me doing it, don't you?"

Without waiting for an answer, she turned and began working over the ice block in the sink. He leaned against the wall of the cramped kitchen and lit a cigarette, exhaling smoke luxuriantly.

"I told you you'd start smoking again." He could sense her smile. Ice chips flew. "Can I have one too?"

He gave her the cigarette he was smoking, then lit another one for himself.

"Thank you," she whispered. Then she turned back to the ice, the edge of the spike slicing into it.

He took two glasses from the cabinet and placed them on the counter, then busied himself with the seal on the bottle of bourbon.

"What did you pay Nilsen for my file?"

Catherine didn't look at him. "Isn't he the policeman you shot last night, Shooter?" She dumped a handful of ice shards in each glass, took the bottle from him and poured the mahogany liquid over them.

"What if I ask you not to call me Shooter?"

"Then what should I call you?" She thought for a moment, then answered her own question. "What if I call you Nicky? How would that be?"

Nick Curran shifted uneasily. "My wife used to call me that."

She smiled knowingly. "I know, but I like it. Nicky." She spoke his name carefully, as if trying it out, getting her tongue used to it. Then she handed him a drink.

"Cheers. *My* friends call me Catherine." She clinked her glass against his.

"What do your lawyers call you?"

"Miss Tramell. The younger ones call me Ms. Tramell."

"What did Manny Vasquez call you?"

"Bitch, mostly—but he meant it affectionately." For a second, a squall of pain seemed to race across her clear blue eyes, but passed quickly. "You don't have any coke, do you? I love coke with Jack Daniel's."

"There's a Pepsi in the fridge," said Nick.

Catherine Tramell smiled and shook her head slightly. "It's just not the same thing, is it?"

"Don't you mean it's not the real thing?" He moved in closer, their bodies almost touching. He could smell her perfume, feel her breath on his cheek. "Where's it going?" he asked quietly. "What do you want from me?"

Their faces were close together now, her face turned up to his, her lips parted. "Say 'what do you want from me, Catherine.'"

"What the *fuck* do you want from me, Catherine?" He leaned down to kiss her, but she dodged away like a fighter ducking a blow and broke the spell.

"Look! I brought you something," she said brightly. She burrowed in her purse and dug out a paperback book, handing it to him. It was *The First Time* by Catherine Woolf.

He studied the cover for a moment.

"Thank you. What's it about?"

"It's about a boy who kills his parents."

"Really? How?"

"They have a plane. The plane crashes. He makes it look like an accident. Fools everybody, particularly the police, but *he* knows. It's his little secret."

He gazed at her intently. "Why does he do it?"

"To see if he can get away with it," she said simply. "It's a game."

"When did you write it?"

"You mean, did I write it *before* my parents died?"

"That's exactly what I mean."

She shook her head, tossing her golden hair. "No. I wrote it years afterward." She put down her drink. She had hardly touched hers. His was half finished.

"Leaving? So soon?"

"Things to do, Nicky." She flashed her smile at him. "Now, you're not going to stop following me around now, are you, just because you're on leave?"

"Absolutely not."

"Good. I'd miss you." She started toward the door. "Of course, I wouldn't want you to get in trouble."

"I'll risk it," he said.

"I'd like to know why you're taking the risk?"

He opened the door for her and she started down the stairs. He leaned on the railing and watched her. "Why risk it? To see if I can get away with it. How's the new book?"

"It's almost writing itself," she said, descending the staircase. Then she stopped and looked back at him. "I'm leaving the house around midnight, in case you're going to be following me."

"Why not make it really easy and tell me where you're going?"

"I'm going down to Johnny's club."

"I'll meet you there," he said, heading back into his apartment and closing the door behind him.

At the bottom of the stairs she met Gus entering the building. When he saw her, he did a double take so theatrical it could only be genuine.

"Hi, Gus!" she said brightly, breezing past him.

He could only gape after her.

By the time he huffed and puffed up the three flights of stairs, Catherine Tramell had jumped into her Lotus and zoomed away, but Nick Curran still stood at the window. He had watched her depart.

"Forgive me for asking, son, and I don't mean to belabor the obvious," said Gus from the doorway, "but I just met that bad-news broad on the steps and it occurs to me to ask why it is that you've got your head so far up your ass?"

Nick was still staring into the street. "She wants to play," he said, as if to himself. "Fine. I can play."

"Everybody she plays with, Nicky, they end up dead."

Nick nodded to himself and thought of his wife, Cindy, dying on their bed, poisoned by her own hand and by her inability to cope with the self-destruction of the man she loved.

"Did you hear me? I said—"

"I heard what you said, Gus."

"Do you know what I mean? Did you understand? Nick, please," he pleaded. "Don't play with her. You can't win against a chick like that. Everybody she fucks with dies, understand?"

Nick Curran tore his eyes from the empty street and looked at his partner. "Understand? Yeah, I understand. I know exactly what that's like."

CHAPTER THIRTEEN

The new sobriety, nineties-style, had been born in San Francisco, but it hadn't yet infected all of the population. There was still a thriving club scene in the city, where patrons got legally stoned on alcohol and music and illicitly zonked on a variety of drugs purveyed in the streets and consumed in club bathrooms.

South of Market, SOMA in clubland parlance, was now the area of choice for the hottest clubs. South of Market Street had once been a dilapidated neighborhood of tumbledown warehouses and rusting industrial facilities, but no longer. It hadn't taken long for someone to figure out that SOMA comprised the largest area of cheap land close to downtown San Francisco. Gentrification had been swift, if not all-encompassing, and the area was now home to dozens of hip clubs, restaurants, bars, and boutiques.

In all of San Francisco, the best known

and most modish clubs were DV8, Slims,
The Warfield (contained in a former theater), and the Oasis, which boasted its own
swimming pool. The gay chic went to the
Trocadero Transfer.

Gay and straight met at Johnny's place,
Altar. Like the once hip Limelight in New
York, Altar was housed in a deconsecrated
church. A deejay spun disks at a booth
where the devout had once taken commu-
nion, and he blasted out music into the
cavernous nave where a thousand dancers
crowded onto the floor.

There was an almost physical presence in
the ear-splitting music. It buffeted Nick as
he came through the front door of the building and into the club proper. The clamor
battered him like a gale force wind and he
felt he had to shoulder his way through it.
The air was heavy with the smell of smoke
and sweat mingled with perfume. The dancers on the floor thrashed to the music, some
of them grim faced and desperate to pound
in abandon into the night hours. They
danced as if determined to have a good time.

The drinkers at the bar drank to get
drunk. There was no conversation—the music
was too loud for that—and if you wanted to
speak to someone you had to beckon his ear
to your mouth and shriek.

Nick managed to get a plastic cup of Jack
Daniel's over ice, stopping just short of yell-
ing himself hoarse, and then circled the
dance floor staring into the mass of bodies,

looking for Catherine Tramell. It was diz-
zying watching that mob which was like a
giant hydra-headed body. Then in the midst
of the crowd, he spotted a familiar face. A
beautiful face he took a moment to place. It
was Roxy.

She was dancing with another woman, her
arms clasped around her partner's waist.
Roxy leaned over and said something to the
girl and she laughed and nodded. Arm in
arm, they made their way off the dance
floor, threading through the packed bodies.
Nick followed.

They were headed for the men's room,
though at Altar the term "men's room" was
not as exclusive as you might imagine. The
men's room was housed in what was once
the sacristy and it was by no means restricted
to men.

It was a dark and shadowy room, the air
heavy with the smells of smoke—tobacco
and that of various controlled substances—
and Nick felt the fetid air rank and clammy
on his lungs. He knew all the smells: crack,
hash, marijuana, and tart hints of coke being
freebased somewhere in one of the stalls.
There were men and women clustered in
the spectral shadows, bending over the various proffered drugs. Discarded, glass crack
vials and used poppers were scattered under-
foot and they crackled like hoarfrost as he
walked into the room.

Roxy rapped on the door of one of the
stalls and it swung open. Catherine Tramell

stood there. Her hair was up and her makeup was as severe as Roxy's. In the shadowy light she looked younger than her thirty years. If Nick hadn't known better, he would have figured her for a youngster like Roxy's companion. A nineteen-year-old, a hot nineteen, a flash-trash nineteen-year-old getting her thrills early in life.

Catherine was not alone in the toilet stall. She stood with her arms around a tall black man. He was shirtless and was a big, pumped-up body builder, his torso sculpted from hard flesh.

He held a glass tube of cocaine under Catherine's nose. She inhaled lustily. There was a little crust of coke on the rim of the vial and she darted out her tongue to scoop it up.

She caught sight of Nick and smiled, at the same time whispering something to her burly companion. He followed the direction of her gaze, looking at Nick and smiling at him, his eyes full of amusement and contempt, then closed the door.

He could wait. Nick Curran wandered through the club, biding his time, checking the place out. He was at once repelled and fascinated by the action. In the dim corners of the club, shadowy figures kissed and groped, men with men, girls with girls, an admixture of sexes in the dark alcoves of Altar.

The music continued to pulsate, bruising the rank air. The stampede on the dance floor never missed a beat. Something between torment and bliss flashed on sweaty faces. The night, the city, the whole world had been compressed into that one electrifying space. There had been no past; there seemed no chance of a tomorrow. There was only the here and now. The present, the future was measured in the seconds between the next dance partner, the minutes before the next drink or hit of cocaine. The music passed seamlessly from track to track, the rhythm and cadence never letting up for a moment.

Then he saw her again. Nick Curran stared as she moved to the music. She was dancing with Roxy and the black body builder. She stood between them, the focus of both. Their lust, as well as the music, seemed to fill her, powering her frenzied dancing.

She turned and saw him and continued to dance, watching him watch her with hungry, famished, fevered eyes. She was teasing him, inserting herself close and warmly between her two cavorting partners. They sandwiched her between their gorgeous bodies, grinding their hips against her.

She took their veneration as her due, but her eyes swept Nick's body, reading him as she had the first time she laid eyes on him. She swayed between her partners, rubbing against them but playing to him with her body.

He felt a wave of craving wash over him.

Suddenly, the whole atmosphere of the club infused itself in his veins like a virus, he too was swept up in the pure, pagan hedonism of the place and its patrons. He was on the dance floor, no longer an observer but a participant. Almost in a trance, he approached her and stood in front of her, devouring her with his eyes. The music throbbed and pulsed.

Catherine stopped dancing and faced him, square-on, challenging in her own way. This challenge he accepted. He reached for her, gathering her up in his arms. She melted into them, kissing him hot and deep.

He held her by the back of the neck, kissing back, his tongue slicing into her mouth. Their bodies pressed hard, as if sealed together. His hands were on her hard ass now, pulling her against him, their hips thrusting. His hands were under her skirt, hot on her bare skin.

She kissed his ear and whispered, "Let's go."

They left Roxy on the dance floor, staring after them with cold fury in her ice-blue eyes.

CHAPTER FOURTEEN

They were in the bedroom of her town house, two naked bodies sprawled on the big, brass bed, their heated lovemaking reflected in a dozen mirrors, glittering in mirrors on the walls and on the ceiling.

He was on top of her, pressing her down with his weight, his cock buried deep within, hips thrusting hard. Nick's tongue snaked across her shoulders to her neck, then down to the furrow between her breasts. Then his lips closed over a nipple, sucking it into his mouth.

She writhed under him, lost in the pure brute carnality of the love they were making. Catherine arched her back and ground her breast into his mouth, crying out, a high, birdlike cry when his teeth took the nipple and bit hard.

Catherine's legs were spread wide and open, her calves locked behind his back like a belt buckle. Her hands were twisted into talons, the red nails digging in and raking the skin on his back, clawing bloody tracks. The harder he thrust, the more vicious her gashes, but the pain and the pleasure comingled and buzzed like a drug in his whirring brain. Blood trickled down his back in warm, salty rivulets and splashed on the white sheets.

She pulled herself from under him and rolled over onto her stomach, presenting herself to him. He reached down and lifted her by her hips. He knelt behind her and kissed her back, his tongue racing down the sprung steel of her spine. Then he was in her again and she bucked as he plunged, piercing her.

Catherine was atop him next, leaning close over his face, her tongue in his mouth. She moved his arms above his head, thrusting her breasts into his face as she stirred. From beneath one of the pillows she took a white silk scarf, dangling it in his face, teasing, daring him to submit to a game which might end in death or ecstasy.

Her eyes questioned; his eyes answered. She nodded and started tying his hands to the brass frame, loosely but firmly. She licked her lips, savoring his helplessness. For a moment, he felt a heady mixture of fear and euphoria. She slid her hips back down onto him, seeming to draw him into her, grinding forcefully. Her head arched back, her breasts high and taut. He strained toward her, thrusting his hips up and deep. Suddenly they were coming together. She breathed deeply and pitched forward onto his chest, her hair tumbling down into his face, a golden canopy enveloping them both. He could feel her body shivering with pleasure, trembling with the delirium that had pulsated through her.

In the still, dark, deep of the night he awoke. There was no sound and just the light from the street reflecting and reflecting again in the mirrors. He swung to the side of the bed and sat for a moment, his head down like an exhausted animal. He passed a hand over his back and felt the tender flesh and the crusts of dried blood. Catherine was curled and asleep. He stretched and stood, picking his way through the wreckage of the room.

The bright light in the bathroom hit Nick like a blow from a hammer. He looked pale and drawn, the flesh around his eyes loose and sallow.

"Christ," he said to his own reflection.

The water from the tap was cold and refreshing. He doused his sweat-matted hair with the frosty water and immediately felt his brain clear a little.

A voice behind him said quietly, "If you don't leave her alone, I'll kill you." There was a matter-of-factness that suggested that Roxy meant every word she said.

Nick glanced at her reflection in the bathroom mirror. "Tell me something, Roxy, man-to-man." He turned and faced her. She didn't even bother to look down at his genitals. "Tell me," he said, "I think she's the fuck of the century, don't you?"

"You make me sick," she said, turning away.

Nick laughed shortly. "*I* make *you* sick?" He shook his head, as if unable to quite believe what he had heard. "You like to watch, don't you? How long were you there, Roxy?"

Roxy stared at him with aversion. "She likes me to watch."

"Just following orders, huh, Roxy?"

"Fuck you," she said, stalking away.

Catherine was hovering in that gray area between sleep and wakefulness. She rubbed against him as he slipped back into the bed, stroking her body against his, like a cat.

"Nicky," she murmured, like a child reassuring herself with her daddy's name.

When he awoke, she was gone. The room had been tidied and light poured through the tall windows.

On the bedside table was a note. "The beach—C."

He took a long, hot, invigorating shower, dressed and then got in his Mustang and drove leisurely out to Stinson Beach. He felt relaxed and powerful in the way that only a night of passionate lovemaking could make him feel. And yet he felt uneasy, unsure of the reception that awaited him.

Catherine was outside as if expecting him. She was, as usual, looking out to sea.

"Morning," he said.

She nodded at him as if he was nothing more than an acquaintance, someone she knew only casually. He glanced at the house and saw one of the curtains twitch, catching a glimpse of Roxy.

"I guess she's not taking this too well."

"Who's not taking what?"

"Roxy. Us."

"She's seen me fuck plenty of guys." She paused a moment, then added, "And there is no 'us.' "

"How do you know? She seems to. Maybe she saw something she hasn't seen before."

Catherine turned to face him, her eyes flashing. "Roxy has seen *everything* before."

Nick chuckled. "I thought *I'd* seen everything."

Her smile softened, becoming a little more friendly. "Did you think it was so special?"

Nick grinned. "I am on record as calling it the fuck of the century."

"Already bragging to your buddies?"

"No, bragging to yours. Roxy."

"How did she take it?"

"Not good. What did *you* think? Of last night?"

"I thought it was a pretty good beginning."

"That's all? How about Roxy? Is she more fun?"

She smiled that knowing smile of hers. "You seem pretty interested in Roxy. Does that mean you'd like her to join us sometime?"

"Did she join you and Johnny?" Nick shot back.

"No. Johnny felt intimidated." ·

Nick shrugged. "And look what happened to him."

Catherine walked away from him, starting toward a path that lead down the side of the rocky bluffs to the beach below. He hurried after her.

"Tell me, Nicky," she called over her shoulder. "Were you frightened last night?"

Nick stopped on the path. "That was the point, wasn't it? That's what made it so good, isn't it?"

"You shouldn't play this game," Catherine said seriously. She started down the path, toward the beach again.

Nick followed. "Why not? I like this game."

"You're in over your head, Nicky. It's not going to come out the way you want it to."

"I may be in over my head. I don't care. This is how I'll catch my killer."

She shook her head. "You won't learn anything from me. I don't confess all my secrets just because I have an orgasm—"

"—or two."

She smiled. "Or two. But you'll never learn anything I don't want you to know."

He seized her shoulders. "Yes I will. And then I'll nail you."

"No. You'll just end up falling in love with me, Nick, that's all."

"I'm already in love with you." She tried to turn away but he held her. "But I'll nail you anyway. You can put that in your book."

CHAPTER FIFTEEN

The Wagon Wheel is a country-and-western bar at Fourteenth and Valencia, a place with a good jukebox and cheap draft beer. Two things that made the place a natural hangout for Gus Moran when he was in his cowboy mode.

Nick Curran found his partner at the bar, folded over a frosted mug of Anchor Steam. Like many of the other patrons in the bar, Gus was dressed for the part in blue jeans, cowboy shirt, and Stetson hat. He was staring moodily at his beer.

Nick slipped onto the stool next to Gus's and took the hat off his partner's head and put it on his own. "Figured I'd find you here," he said.

"You're fuckin' perky tonight." He twisted around on the stool. "Where the fuck you been, anyway? I went over to your place. Nothing." Gus was talking loudly, too loudly, and slurring his words. He was one, possibly two, drinks away from total inebriation.

"Easy there, partner. I wasn't home, that's all."

"I went over last night, too."

"I wasn't there last night, either."

Gus took a long pull on his beer and stared hard at his partner, looking as if he was trying to unravel a knotty problem and his drink-hazed brain was not cooperating. Finally, he got it. His face darkened. "You . . . *fucked* her! Goddamn dumb sonofabitch! You weren't home because you were off banging that goddamn broad! I can't believe it! Are you completely crazy? '

"Simmer down, Gus. Don't get so bent out of shape about it. It's nothing I can't handle."

"Bullshit! Goddamn, you are one dumb sonofabitch and I am getting out of here because you're bad luck and it's catching. And I don't need no more bad luck. Got all I can handle, thank you very much." He got off his bar stool and started staggering toward the door.

"Don't worry about it. Next time I'll use a rubber."

You can never be sure just what will annoy a drunk. For some reason the reference to rubbers infuriated Gus and he wasn't shy about letting Nick, and the whole bar, know it. Very loudly and slowly he said, "I don't give a flyin' chili bean fart about rubbers, Curran!"

"Hey Gus!" The bartender was shouting after him, waving a bill. "Think maybe you're forgetting something?" He was glad to see Gus go, but he wasn't about to get stiffed.

Nick took care of it. He turned back to the bar. "How much?"

"Seventeen," said the bartender.

"Drinks or bucks?"

"Bucks."

Nick slapped a twenty on the bar. "Keep the change."

He caught up with Gus Moran on the sidewalk in front of the Wagon Wheel. He was staring at two middle-aged women, both of them dressed in country-western gear. They were headed for the bar, but Gus stood between them and the door.

"Rubbers," announced Gus.

"You really have to protect yourself," said Nick, "It's something you should be thinking about."

"What the hell for? Do you really think I'm getting any at my age?"

"Sure."

Gus waved tipsily at the two overage cowgirls. "I mean, sure, I can get laid ... by goddamn *blue* hairs like those two. But I don't like 'em, you know, Nicky. I just don't *like* 'em."

"That's a problem," said Nick, hustling Gus away from the two offended women and down the street.

"Where the hell are you taking me?"

"Time to sober up a little. Get a little cof-

fee in you, a little something to eat—you'll
feel like a million bucks in no time."

"I am a little peckish, at that," Gus said
thoughtfully.

Mac's was a real, honest-to-goodness, all-
night diner. It was on Mason Street, close to
the San Francisco theater district and the
seedy Tenderloin. It drew a mix of theatergoers, cops, cabbies, and tourists and that
night every stool at the counter was filled.
Gus stared at a fat woman at the counter.
She was a tourist, that much was obvious
from Fisherman's Wharf T-shirt. For a
moment Gus looked like he was going to say
something to her, something, no doubt,
pretty offensive. Nick guided him into a
booth and sat him down.

The food at Mac's was good and the coffee
was better. Nick did his best to see that his
partner got more than his fair share of it.
He also ordered him a huge plate of eggs
and a side order of chili topped with Jack
cheese and a mound of sour cream.

"Eat," Nick commanded.

Gus ate, guzzling the grease and slurping
his coffee. For a few minutes the only noise
at the table was the sound of him eating.

"Feeling better?"

"I feel *fine!*" The loud tone of voice suggested that Gus might still have been the
tiniest bit smashed.

"Shh," said Nick.

"Don't shush me," Gus said irately. "Don't

you ever shush me, sonny boy." He shoveled a forkful of chili and egg into his mouth. "How could you fuck her?"

People were looking over at him now, throwing angry glances in his direction. Gus didn't seem to notice, or, if he did, didn't care.

"You wanna die, son? What is it? Still all screwed-up about those fuckin' tourists? You still feel bad about something that happened to you years ago. You feel so bad about it you're wiggling your way onto an ice pick. That's what you got planned, right?"

"Gus, that's not—"

Gus raised his voice. "We got too many goddamn tourists comin' in here anyway. Plenty more goddamn tourists where they goddamn came from."

"Gus, c'mon."

"I'm mad at you, sonny, real mad. And you wanna know why? I'll tell you. Because you don't have the sense to be scared of that woman. You're not scared of her, are you?"

"No," said Nick quietly. "I'm not afraid of her."

"Why the hell not?" Gus demanded.

Nick shook his head slowly. "I don't know. I'm just not afraid of her."

"That's her pussy talking to you, sonny. It's all about pussy."

The fat tourist at the counter put down her hamburger and shot an ugly glance at Gus. He grinned at her and winked.

"No, it isn't," Nick insisted.

"Yes, it is. You're listening to her pussy. Because I know you ain't listening to your own brain."

"I know what I'm doing."

"No you don't." Gus drank some more coffee and settled the cowboy hat on his head. "Listen up, sonny. Internal Affairs did a track on Martin D-for-Dickhead Nilsen. All in all, pretty interesting."

"What did they find out?"

"Don't rush me. Very interesting, like I said, and the shooflies are doing their damndest to make sure that no one outside of their nest hears about it. But ol' Gus, friend to all, enemy to none, got to hearing about it."

"Heard what?"

"That IA found a safety deposit box with fifty thousand dollars in it. He rented it three months ago. Been there once. Put the money in and never went back. Me, I'da been visiting it every couple of days, you know what I mean?" He leered obscenely at the fat woman, really giving her the eye.

"But that doesn't make sense. She didn't even know me three months ago."

"Maybe it wasn't her that paid him. You're in Internal Affairs, the chances for going on the pad are plenty thick on the ground. After all, who's gonna be looking at you? You're in IA, you don't have to worry about IA. Am I right or am I right?"

"She paid him."

Gus Moran shrugged. "Well, what the fuck do I know about it anyway? I'm just an old city cowboy tryin' not to fall out of his saddle."

"C'mon, let's get the hell out of here."

"Okay, pardner."

When they made it to Gus's battered 1980 Seville, he had a certain amount of trouble getting the door unlocked. Clearly, the man was not in any shape to drive.

"You want me to drive you? You know what they say about friends not letting friends—"

"I ain't drunk."

"I know that. I just thought you might want me to drive you home so you don't have to worry about it."

"In that piss-ant car of yours? Hell, no. I ain't gettin' no back pain disability retirement. I'm gettin' me a full pension and a real gold-plate genuine Seiko watch."

Gus had a point. The front seat of the ancient, rust-eaten Caddy was as wide and as comfy as a living-room couch. The Mustang was cramped.

"Come on, I'll drive you in this thing."

Gus looked deeply offended. "This 'thing,' sonny, happens to be a Cadillac car. You think I'd let you drive my Cadillac car? I ain't lettin' no crazy pain in the ass like you driving my Cadillac car."

"Gus—"

"Fuck off, sonny, I'm outta here." He slung himself into the car and fired up the big engine. He revved it a couple of times like a dragster, then popped the clutch, zooming out of the parking lot, laying rubber and leaving a smoke trail behind him. Three blocks away Nick Curran could still hear the engine and the squeal of brakes from the old Cadillac. He shook his head and hoped Gus would get home in one piece.

Slowly he walked to his own car. He replayed Gus's words over and over in his brain, thinking about Nilsen and Catherine Tramell. How had she made the connection? How had she known that he would have been able to get his hands on Nick's file? Of course, there was no proof that she actually had gotten the file from Nilsen. The only answer he easily came to was a motive for Nilsen's actions: He sold the file because he hated Nick Curran. The money was just gravy, a little extra.

Nick was so deep in thought that he didn't notice a car tracking just behind him, following him. He didn't notice it until the driver gunned the engine and tried to run him down.

There's no sound quite like a Lotus engine on full bore. The black car rocketed down the narrow alley like an artillery shell, blasting toward him. Nick caught a quick glimpse of the machine as it hit him and tossed him over the hood and body of the sleek car. The driver slammed on the brakes and the Lotus screeched to a halt. The car engine roared as the gears were ground into reverse and hurtled backward toward Nick.

He leaped out of its path, scrambled to the Mustang as the Lotus tried one more time to hit him.

The driver of the car—Catherine?—decided that two attempts at vehicular homicide were enough for one evening. The car bolted into the street and screamed into a fishtail right turn.

Nick was behind the wheel of his Mustang in seconds and barreling down the alley in hot pursuit. He caught a flash of the powerful black car making a left on Valencia.

The Lotus was making for North Beach, careening through the hilly streets, the big car taking the steep grade effortlessly. It blew across the brightly lit strip of topless bars and porno theaters on Broadway then shot up the hill onto Vallejo, then Kearny, then Green. Nick was right behind her, the engine on the Mustang bellowing power.

The Lotus was on Telegraph Hill now, the highest point in downtown San Francisco, a hill so steep that some of the streets are nothing more than long, long flights of concrete stairs. Nick slammed the Mustang into low and ground the gas pedal into the floor, pointing the screaming automobile up the steps. He was aiming for a choke point on the summit of the hill, a straightaway where he would cut her off.

The Mustang bounced and bucked on the steps, its exhaust and muffler tearing on the concrete, every joint and weld in the frame shrieking, but the tough engine pulled the vehicle to the top of the stairs. He threw it into a tight turn on Kearny.

The lights of the Lotus were headed straight for him now, a game of chicken played out in two high-powered automobiles. Nick was really pounding the gas pedal, blasting head-on for the Lotus. At the last possible moment, her nerve broke and she tried to swerve on the narrow road, but there wasn't room.

Engine screaming, the car hurtled over the side and end-down into a foundation pit for the new Moscone Center. It somersaulted twice and landed on its roof. The engine was dead. And by the time Nick got to the car, so was Roxy. She was slumped, half out of the open door, her neck broken. Not far away, police sirens wailed.

Nick Curran did a very good impersonation of John Q. Citizen, giving a statement to a policeman who laboriously wrote it out in an accident report and then returned it to Nick for his signature.

But it wasn't any ordinary accident. Not many car accidents get the attention of Detectives Sullivan and Morgan of the San Francisco Police Department Internal Affairs Division, or Lieutenant Walker, Homicide Chief.

Walker ripped the statement out of Nick's hands and waved it under his nose.

"This crock of shit is your statement? You're actually going to sign your name to it?"

"Why not?" Nick put a cigarette in his mouth and lit it, waving out the match. "Why shouldn't I? It was an accident."

Walker slapped the statement with the back of his hand, as if trying to punish the words written there. "Let me get this straight, Curran. You're driving around North Beach for no particular reason and this car won't get out of the way. And you tell me it was an accident?"

"Well, Phil, I don't think she really meant to go over the side, do you?"

"Let me have him for a minute," said Sullivan.

Walker waved the Internal Affairs guy off. "Don't fuck with me, Nick," he said quietly. "I don't need a reason to put your ass in a sling."

Sullivan butted in. "Full name of deceased—Roxanne Hardy. Last address—some shit hole in Cloverdale. No priors, no convictions. The car is registered to Catherine Tramell." He shut his notebook with a snap. "Small world, huh, Curran?"

Walker looked at Nick as if he wanted to kill him then and there. "You knew her, didn't you?"

Nick shrugged. "Gus and I talked to her at Tramell's house. All we did was write her name down."

Walker was on the verge of blowing his

top. "You wrote her name down and then, big surprise! She rolls her car into a pit right in front of you and dies. That's what you're telling me? You expect me to believe it?"

Nick shot his cigarette butt into the dirt. "That's all I know."

"Then fuck you. *Fuck you,* Nick. They can hang you out to dry for all I care." He started to stalk away, then stopped. "Remember, Nick, you did this to yourself. No one to blame but you."

"I'll bear that in mind, Lieutenant."

"I told you to stay away from Tramell. It was an order."

"Yeah, but you didn't tell me to stay away from her car."

"Asshole," muttered Walker.

"You're out of control, Curran," said Sullivan. "I want you in Dr. Garner's office at nine o'clock tomorrow morning."

"Yeah? Who are you guys gonna sell my file to this time? *The National Enquirer*?"

Two morgue attendants were lifting Roxy's body from behind the wheel of the car. Her dead, sightless eyes were open and staring right at Nick.

CHAPTER SIXTEEN

Nick had gone to bed early, sober, and alone, so he looked good and in control when he arrived at Police Headquarters the next morning. Beth was waiting for him in the interrogation room, but she wasn't alone. Sitting next to her at the table were two men, one was short and balding and looked like an accountant. The other was silver-haired and smooth looking, with well-capped teeth and an expensive Rolex on his wrist. Nick had never seen a Hollywood agent, but this guy looked like what he imagined one to be. Both men, however, were psychiatrists, big guns brought in to really give him a third degree headshrinking session. One look at them and already he could feel his anger rising, his control slipping.

"This is Doctor Myron, Nick," said Beth Garner, indicating the accountant type, "and this is Doctor McElwaine."

"Nice names," said Nick sourly.

The three doctors laughed uneasily.

"They've been asked to consult with me on this."

" 'They've been asked'—You mean *you* didn't ask them. They were foisted on you by person or persons unknown in the San Francisco Police Department, is that correct?" Neither doctor made any notes, but you could almost hear them starting their observation: aggressive, hostile, argumentative, antagonistic, resentful of authority.

"They are both eminent doctors, Nick. I value their opinions and expertise. I welcome their assistance."

"Why don't you have a seat," said Doctor Myron.

"Great idea," Nick said nastily. "I'm glad you thought of that, Doc. It never would have occurred to me."

There was another round of uncomfortable laughter. Nick sat and for a long moment the three doctors looked at him. He stared back. Finally McElwaine broke the silence.

"Nick," he said gently, "we understand from Doctor Garner that you have been having a certain amount of trouble controlling your temper of late. Is that so?"

"Only with regard to one person," said Nick.

"Do you think Lieutenant Nilsen deserved to die?" asked Doctor Myron.

"Deserved to die?" Nick shrugged. "I don't make judgments like that."

"But you feel little remorse at his death?"

"Remorse? I would only feel remorse, Doc, if I had something to do with his death. And I didn't. Are you asking if I feel any regrets?" Nick shrugged again. "I didn't know the guy well enough. Let's just say I won't miss him."

"But you do take a certain pleasure in his death? Is that a fair statement?"

"That, Doctor, is a sick statement. No one—no sane person, anyway—ever takes any pleasure in a death. I certainly don't." Nick folded his arms across his chest with an air of finality.

McElwaine shot a worried glance at his colleague and decided to try a different tack. His voice was courtly and avuncular and he smiled warmly, showing his nice white teeth. "Tell me Nick, when you remember your childhood, are your recollections pleasing to you? Or are you disturbed by some of your memories?"

Nick looked at his inquisitor for a full half minute, thirty seconds of anger and disbelief. He managed to keep the rage out of his voice, but not the incredulity.

"Okay," he said calmly, directly. "Number one: I don't remember how often I used to jack off, but it was a lot."

Beth Garner closed her eyes and shook her head. Nick Curran would not control his temper. He would *never* do himself a favor and play ball.

Nick's voice was rising. "Number two: I didn't get pissed off at my dad, even after I was old enough to know what he and mom were doing in the bedroom."

"Nick," whispered Beth, *"please."*

"Let me finish. Number three: I don't look in the toilet before I flush it. Number four: I don't wet the bed and I haven't for some time."

"Nick!" implored Beth.

"And number five: You can go fuck yourselves because I am out of here." Nick stood and stalked from the room.

As he went, he heard Doctor Myron say, "Well!"

Beth was right behind him, running down the hall in an effort to catch up with him. She was angry and hurt at the same time, grabbing him by the sleeve of his jacket, attempting to slow him down.

"What is your problem?" Beth was very close to losing it herself. She fought to control her emotions. "I'm trying to help you. Why won't you let me help you?"

Nick tore his sleeve from her grasp. He continued down the corridor. "I don't want your help. I don't need any help. Do you understand me?"

"Yes, you do," Beth insisted. "Something's going on with you. You're sleeping with her, aren't you."

He stopped walking and turned. "What is this interest you've got in her anyway, Beth? Jealous?"

"My interest is in *you*, not her. She seduces

people. She manipulates them. She'll do anything."

"I thought you hardly knew her."

"I know the type. I'm a psychologist, remember? I've studied people like her. I've analyzed people like her."

"Oh, a psychologist! That means you manipulate people, too, doesn't it, Beth? You're a *practicing* psychologist. That means you're better at it than she is. That's all." He turned and started down the hallway again, but this time Beth Garner didn't follow.

"I feel sorry for you, Nick." She shrugged and walked in the opposite direction. There was nothing more she could do for him.

He got to Catherine Tramell's house at Stinson a little before one in the afternoon. The heavy fog on Highway 1 slowed him down. The mist was thick on the bluffs as well, enshrouding the house and cutting it off from the sea completely.

The house looked deserted, but the white Lotus was parked out front. Even if it hadn't been there, he knew that it was at Stinson that he would find her. Stinson was her refuge, her shelter, bunker, her ivory tower.

She did not answer his knock. Tentatively, unsure of himself, he opened the door. "Catherine?"

There was no answering call.

The house was dark and gloomy, all of the shades drawn against the white glare of the fog. The house seemed suffused in mourning and possessed by a silence so profound it seemed he could reach out his hand and touch it.

He stood in the middle of the darkened hallway and listened. Just beneath the silence there was a sound, a tiny, sliver of noise, a metered creak every few seconds, regular as a clock. He walked along the hallway, following the sound like a gun dog on a trail, stopping every few steps to listen.

Catherine was sitting in a rocking chair in the corner of the living room, pitching gently forward and back on the wooden rockers. She gazed at him with wide, red-rimmed eyes. Her hair was a tangled mess, her cheeks drawn and hollow with lack of sleep. She hadn't slept, that was obvious, and her face was tearstained.

She looked away from him and spoke haltingly. The self-confidence, the calm assurance and self-possession had vanished, replaced by doubt and grief.

"After you left the other day, when you were here at the beach, I came back into the house. She looked at me so strangely. She left right after you." Catherine Tramell raked her nails through her tousled hair. She shook her head slowly. "I shouldn't have allowed her to . . . I shouldn't have let her watch us that night. But she wanted to watch me. She said she always wanted to watch me. All the time."

She turned back to him, looking at him with that same gaze, the one he had seen the first time he had laid eyes on her.

"She tried to kill you, didn't she, Nick."

He didn't reply right away. "Did you like her watching you?"

"Do you think I told her to kill you?"

He had decided that he knew the answer to that question already. He shook his head. "No, I don't think you had anything to do with it."

She looked out to sea. "Everybody I care about . . . dies."

He knelt behind her and put his hands on her shoulders, kneading them under his strong fingers. She shivered at his touch. His hands slid down, spreading open her shirt, gently caressing her breasts.

"I'm not dead," he said.

She rubbed her face against his arm, like a cat begging for its owner's attention. "Please," she said, "please make love to me."

The only light in the living room came from the fireplace. A drenching cold rain off the Pacific pounded on the shingled roof of the house and whipped at the windows. Their lovemaking had been intense, as potent as before, but without the pain and gameplaying. It had been the soothing, pacifying love of lovers, not the frenzied, lustful one-upmanship of erotic rivals.

Catherine lay nestled in his arms, satisfied, but also invaded by the melancholy that sometimes follows lovemaking, with the return to the real world.

She was silent for a long time, then whispered, "What are you thinking about?"

"I was thinking . . . I was thinking that I was wrong."

"Wrong? About what?"

"About you. About Roxy."

"Roxy?"

He kissed her forehead lightly. "I think she may have killed Boz."

Catherine started slightly, as if he had pinched her. "Killed Johnny? Why? To set me up? She wouldn't have done a thing like that. She loved me. She wouldn't want to hurt me. To frame me, like that."

"She was jealous of me. Maybe she was jealous of Johnny, too."

"She wasn't," Catherine said firmly. "That wasn't like her. She never got jealous. Not before you, anyway. She got excited."

Nick shrugged. "It's a shame we won't be able to ask her about it."

Catherine rolled over, her head on his shoulder, her hair splashed across his chest in a golden pool. "I don't have luck with women."

Nick grinned. "You and me both. 'Til now, that is."

She ignored his flippancy. "There was a girl. When I was in college, I slept with her once. She went around—" Catherine put her hand to her mouth, as if trying to stop herself from saying more.

"What happened to her?" asked Nick. "What did she do? Did she hurt you?"

Catherine Tramell shook her head. "No, not physically. She became obsessed with me. She went around taking pictures of me. She dyed her hair. She copied my clothes. She followed me. Lisa something, her name was. Lisa Oberman." She shuddered at the recollection. "It was awful."

Nick stroked her hair, as if calming a child wrenched awake by a nightmare. "I thought you didn't make confessions," he said tenderly.

She looked into his eyes. "I never have. Not before this."

Daylight was streaming through the windows when Nick Curran awoke. He was alone and the name "Lisa Oberman" buzzed in his mind, as persistent as a fly at a screen door. He rolled over, half expecting to find a note on the table telling him that Catherine had returned to the city, but there was none. He lay very still and listened. There was no sound in the house, only the endless pummeling of the breakers on the beach.

Nick got up and pulled on his pants and shirt and went in search of her. She was not in the house, nor was she on the veranda keeping her vigil over the waves. The Lotus was in the driveway. She couldn't have gone far.

He followed the rocky path down to the beach and found it deserted. He peeked into the small beach house, a cabana which stood a few feet from the shoreline. No sign of her. But he was confident she would turn up eventually. He sighed and looked out to sea, turning his face to the sun, relaxed and content.

Then someone hit him hard from behind. Nick reacted fast, slinging his attacker over his shoulder and down hard onto the sand. He dropped rapidly, his knee pointed for his assailant's throat.

"Nick!" yelled Catherine. "Stop!" She was sprawled in the sand, laughing and fearful at the same time.

Nick exhaled heavily, relieved that he had been the victim of her horseplay, not an attack.

"Man!" she said with a laugh. "Are you jumpy!"

He hated to admit to himself the truth of her words. "Still playing games, is that it?"

She rocked her head on the sand. "No more games. The games are over. Get off me. Let me up."

Nick lifted his weight off her and helped her up, brushing sand off her blue jeans. Catherine whipped her hair around, like a dog shedding water. They started back up the beach toward the house. Then she stopped and dropped into one of the cane chairs outside the cabana. "No more games," she said, "that's a promise."

"A promise? Then tell me about Nilsen."

Her eyes were bright with mirth. "I'd tell you, but I know you won't believe me."

"Try me."

Catherine shrugged. "I saw his name in the *Chronicle* articles about you. I contacted him and we struck a bargain. Fifty thousand dollars—cash, he was very specific about that—and in return I got your file. Your police record, your psychiatric profile. Everything. The works." She spoke matter-of-factly.

His features had hardened. "When?"

"About three months before I met you."

"Why?"

"I knew about you from the papers. I'd read about the shooting. I was intrigued. I decided to write a book about a detective. A detective a lot like you."

"I'd say he sounded exactly like me."

"I wanted to know about my character," she said hotly. "That's all."

"You paid fifty thousand dollars for your *character*?" asked Nick in disbelief.

She was unapologetic. The vulnerability of the night before had been replaced by her usual cocksuredness. "I would have paid more. I wanted to know everything about you. Then you came down here after Johnny got killed. It gave me a chance to get to know my character better."

"What about the other night?" Nick demanded. "What about *last* night? Was that just research? Maybe all you were doing was getting to know your character a little better."

She studied his face for a long moment, then looked away. "Maybe I'm losing interest in my book, my character. Maybe I'm learning to like the real thing."

"Is that true?"

"Don't you believe me?"

"I don't know," Nick said.

"I'll convince you."

She put her arms around him and kissed him slowly. The heat of the kiss shimmered on his lips. Nick felt a sudden surge of arousal pulse through him and he held her tight and kissed her back deeply.

Catherine tried to pull away when the cordless phone in the cabana started ringing, but he held her. "Let it go," he murmured.

She broke from him and answered the phone, listening for only a moment before passing the receiver to Nick. "It's for you," she said.

"Who is it?"

"It's Gus. Gus-who-doesn't-like-me. That Gus."

He took the phone and she entwined herself around him, kissing his face lightly as he tried to talk to his partner.

"Catherine says you don't like her, Gus. I can't believe it, can you?"

"She's right," snapped Gus. "You got an ice pick in you yet?"

Nick rubbed his hands over his body, as if checking himself for deep puncture wounds. "Nope, not yet."

"What did he say?" asked Catherine.

"He asked if I had an ice pick in me yet."

"Funny," said Catherine.

"She didn't think it was funny, Gus."

"Like I give a shit what she thinks. You know that stuff they say about how you can judge people by their friends, Nicky?"

"I don't believe it," said Nick.

"Yeah? Why not?"

Nick grinned. "*You're* my friend, Gus."

"You better start believing it, my friend, because I'm gonna make you see the folly of your ways."

"Yeah? How are you planning to do that."

"Because, Nick Pain-in-the-Ass Curran, you just won yourself an all expenses paid, round-trip ticket to a fascinating crime scene."

Nick felt shock jolt through him. "Jesus Christ. Who now, Gus?"

"Gotcha scared, huh, sonny? Relax, it's nobody now. Happened a long time ago. But I believe it's germane. Like that, Nicky? 'Germane.' "

"Where is this fascinating, germane crime scene?"

"In exotic Cloverdale, sonny. So get in your piece-of-shit kiddy car and zoom up beautiful 101 to Cloverdale. I'll meet you at the police headquarters there in two hours." Gus chuckled and then he slammed down the phone.

CHAPTER
SEVENTEEN

If Cloverdale wasn't *the* dullest, most quiet town in Northern California, it was certainly in the top ten. It was in Sonoma County, and was the last big town before Mendocino County. Unlike other Sonoma towns like Geyserville and Healdsburg and Sonoma itself, there was nothing cute or trendy about Cloverdale. Sonoma County was famous as a wine-producing area. Many of the towns and villages had that faintly European air that usually goes with vineyard towns—good restaurants, trendy shops. But there is no viticulture in Cloverdale. The major industry is dairy products, and the only thing that distinguished the town at all was the fact that Highway 101, the unlovely north-south artery, was also the town's main street. It was lined with a motley collection of truck stops and fast food places, strip malls and motels. All in all, Cloverdale seemed an unlikely place for a murder. Particularly a murder as peculiar as the one Gus had uncovered there.

Nick was nearing the outskirts of the town when he realized that he had heard something about Cloverdale recently. It was the night of his dangerous duel with Roxy driving the Lotus. One of the Internal Affairs guys had identified Roxy as . . . Roxanne Hardy. And Nick could almost hear Sullivan's voice: "Roxanne Hardy. Last known address—some shit hole in Cloverdale. No priors, no convictions." This sudden and unexpected trip to upper Sonoma County had to have something to do with her.

Nick found Gus outside the police station on the town's main drag. He was leaning against the crumpled fender of his big, old, Cadillac, eating a greasy fajita, purchased at one of the roadside stands in beautiful downtown Cloverdale.

"Nice of you to come, sonny." Gus Moran crumpled up the grease-paper wrapping of the fajita and tossed it away. It wasn't that he didn't believe in keeping America beautiful. It was just that he realized it was too late for Cloverdale.

"What's this about, Gus? I mean, what is this about *besides* Roxy."

Gus wagged his finger at Nick. "What a smart guy I got for a partner. Figured it out, all by your little lonesome, right?"

"Everything except what the fuck we're doing here."

"Well, lemme guess, sonny. I bet you spent last night humpin' that Catherine

Tramell, right? Well, while you were humpin' her, I was back at headquarters humpin' that lousy computer and I turned up some stuff. Stuff I'm not supposed to be sharing with you, but what the hell. I figured it was sorta like a good-bye present."

"Good-bye? Where am I going?"

"That decision will be made, Nicky, right after that crazy broad sticks a nice, sharp ice pick into your throat. Heaven, hell—I can't say. But I can guess."

"You are a barrel of laughs this morning, Gus."

"Yeah, that's one thing dames like about me, my sense of humor." He started up the steps of the police station. "C'mon now Nick, lets not keep the nice policeman waiting."

It turned out that they were meeting a policewoman, a sergeant named Janet Cushman who headed up a three-person juvenile crime office for Cloverdale township. The Roxanne Hardy case had been before her time, but Cushman knew all about it.

"Biggest thing that ever happened in juvey," she said, "in this town anyway. Before this came down all the juvenile crime was penny-ante—joyriding in stolen cars, cracking open candy machines, that kind of thing. Right out of the 1950s." Both Nick and Gus nodded understandingly. In their teens they had done their fair share of juvenile delinquency.

"It was because of this case that my division got set up. Right after Roxanne Hardy knocked off her little brothers, everyone was sure that Cloverdale was about to have a juvenile crime wave. So this unit came into being. No homicides. Not yet, anyway. Mostly we're handling abuse cases."

"Could we see the file, Sergeant?" asked Nick.

Cushman already had it out. She shoved it across the desk. "Help yourself. But you can't copy it without permission from the chief."

"No problem," said Nick.

The first thing he fished out of the dun-colored folder was a black-and-white crime-scene photograph of two little boys lying in what appeared to be a mud puddle in a garden. The mud was a pool of the boys' own blood and the crime-scene photographer had been scrupulous about getting a good, clear shot of the gaping slash wounds on the thin necks.

Nick had a wide experience of corpses, in the flesh and in glossy, glaring, merciless photographs like this one. But there was something about this one that made him slightly queasy. It was the violence of child against child in a suburban garden. The victims were about seven and nine years old. There was a picture of Roxy, too, but this one hadn't been taken by a police photographer. This had been lifted from a family album. It showed a girl in braids, braces on her teeth, smiling at the lens of someone's old Kodak.

"How old was she when she did this?" he asked Cushman.

"Fourteen. Like I say, the biggest juvey crime ever. She would have had to wait four years to kill them if she wanted to get tried as an adult."

Nick was puzzled. "But Sullivan said that she had no priors and no convictions."

"She was never arrested. She was never tried. They sent her away to a special home. Like a little Atascadero—just for kids." Atascadero was the California State home for the criminally insane.

"I didn't turn this up on the priors file," Gus explained. "It took a little creative thinking. I ran it through the state Health and Human Services file, looking for mentions of Roxanne Hardy as a ward of the state."

"How'd you happen to know to do that, Gus?"

"How? Because she was a fuckin' whack job, that's how I happened to know to do that, sonny. I figured she'd show up somewhere in the state whack-job records. Shit, I had nothing else to do last night," he said with a shrug.

"Was there a motive?" Nick asked and instantly felt foolish for having posed the question. It may have been an adult crime, but a kid had committed it. Motive didn't enter into it.

Gus laughed. "Motive? Yeah, she did it for the insurance money."

Janet Cushman didn't think it was a laughing matter. She frowned at Gus. "She said she didn't know herself. One minute she was playing romper room with her brothers. The next thing you know she cut their throats with her daddy's straight razor. Just sort of did it on impulse." Cushman shrugged. "The razor just happened to be there."

Gus and Nick stared at her. They had heard that story before, the same story from a sweet old lady named Hazel Dobkins who also happened to be a friend of Catherine Tramell. Gus muttered something under his breath. It sounded very much like "Fuckin' whack jobs."

"Do you want copies?" asked Cushman. "I'll go corral the chief before he goes to lunch."

"Naw," said Nick. "I don't think we need it."

"Thanks, Sergeant," said Gus. "Thanks for your help. I guess we'll be on our way."

They headed out of the police headquarters and back to their cars.

"You know," said Nick, "I don't understand what the hell is going on here."

"Ain't that hard, son. This young farm girl, this here Roxanne Hardy, she got tired of all the attention goin' to her little brothers, so she *fixed* them and she fixed them good. Just like ol' Hazel Dobkins fixed her whole family. Except young Roxy here, she didn't use a wedding present. She used daddy's razor."

"But why?"

Gus leaned against the creased fender of his Cadillac. "Does it matter? Hazel, Roxy, this fine, rich Catherine Tramell—" He shook his head and laughed. "Christ, what a trio. Sure makes you wonder what they talked about when they set themselves down in front of the campfire at night." Shaking his head ruefully, Gus climbed in behind the wheel of his beat-up gas guzzler. "Tell me, sonny, you ever met a friend of hers who *hasn't* killed anybody?" He yanked the door closed. "Well, I guess it takes all kinds. And you gotta admit, it probably beats your ordinary everyday girl talk." He twisted the key in the ignition and the big engine burst into life. "See you later, Nick." The car started to roll away.

"I'm not sure anymore that she did it," said Nick over the growling of the engine.

Gus snorted derisively and looked with eyes full of pity at his young partner. "Which one you talking about now, son? We know ol' Hazel did it; we know young Roxy did it. And the other one: well, hell, she's got that magna-come-lawdy pussy on her that done fried up your brain. Like I said, see you later, sonny." Gus Moran put the car in gear and pulled out into traffic.

Nick followed, trailing behind the battered Cadillac all along Route 101, through Sonoma and into Marin. As the two-car convoy approached San Rafael, Gus Moran gunned away and took the turnoff for the Golden Gate Bridge and San Francisco, getting in line with all the other cars queuing up for bridge access. Without really thinking about it, Nick Curran started in the same direction when a green traffic sign caught his eye: Richmond, Albany, Berkeley—Keep Right.

On impulse, he took the road to the right and Berkeley, home of the University of California's most prestigious campus, the college where Catherine Tramell had done her undergraduate work. Maybe, just maybe, there was something that could be unearthed in her academic past. Conceivably, there was information there too about the strange, tortured college career of Lisa Oberman, the student who had so tormented Catherine in her sophomore year.

The ride from San Rafael to Berkeley has its moments of fine scenery: a beautiful view from the Richmond–San Rafael Bridge of San Pablo Bay to the left and the wide, shimmery expanse of San Francisco Bay to the right. As you look back at San Rafael from the bridge, you can see the canalside million-dollar homes of that tony community, as well as, incongruously, the forbidding bulk of San Quentin prison, sealed off from the expensive homes, shops, and marinas by the *cordon sanitaire* of Interstate 580. Nick had long ago lost count of the number of the men he had sent to The Q, but he did recall that the women's wing had been home to Hazel Dobkins for many years.

Once he was past the Chevron long pier on the Contra Costa side of the bridge, there was no more sightseeing to be done. He tore through the bedroom communities of Richmond and Albany, blew by the racetrack, Golden Gate Fields, and took the turnoff for the main artery leading to the UC campus, University Avenue.

Parts of the city of Berkeley seemed to have been frozen in time—a specific time, the late 1960s. Hippies lingered in the streets, decked out in bib overalls and tie-dyed T-shirts; acres of wall space were covered with peeling posters and manifestos demanding free health care, power to the homeless, denouncing American foreign policy in Central America, Africa, the Middle East. Berkeley was determined to remain the lone outpost of radicalism in the United States, even though there was something faintly old-fashioned about the political stance. Most of the hippies looked like they were in their fifties, and Nick could imagine these grizzled veterans of the counterculture getting together to smoke a joint and reminisce about the glory days of People's Park, the March on Washington, and the Days of Rage, swapping antiwar stories like vets at a VFW Hall.

He parked on Bancroft and made his way onto the campus. Things were a little different here. Although Berkeley, the univer-

sity, still had its fair share of radical
students, most of them were more concerned with their studies. Having won a
place at a great university, they were preoc-
cupied with keeping up with their school
work, getting straight A's and then going on
to the high-paying career of their choice.
The denim and tie-dyed look was less preva-
lent here, the students going more for the
neat and clean preppy look.

There was the usual collection of eccen-
trics and panhandlers in Sproul Plaza, but
they too seemed too old to be students. The
real students stared curiously at the Jews
for Jesus and the guy singing Frank Sinatra
songs at the top of his lungs, then hurried
away to their economics classes.

The campus was pleasant and calm, the
long walks shadowed with stands of tall
eucalyptus trees. Nick enjoyed his walk,
looking at the pretty coeds with an approv-
ing eye. He asked one for directions and
received the information he wanted plus the
bonus of a dazzling smile. If he had the time
and the inclination, he would have invited
the girl for a cup of coffee, but he had work
to do.

Dwinelle Hall, he had been told, was the
main administration building, home of the
registrar and all student records. In a basement office, he showed his police ID and a
woman scarcely out of her teens—Nick
guessed she was probably a work-study student—sat down at a computer and put it on
line.

"I'm looking for information on a former student," he explained. "A Lisa Oberman."

"Do you have a year? The files are arranged by year."

"I'd guess about '82 or '83."

"Guess?" said the young woman. Nick noticed there was a large, fat biology textbook open next to the computer. She probably resented a cop cutting in on her study time. Her fingers danced over the computer keyboard.

"There are lots of Obermans," she said. "Andrea C., Andrew W., . . ." Her eyes scanned the column of names on the screen. "Donald M., Mark W. Sorry, no Lisa Oberman. You're sure about the year?"

"Catherine Tramell said she graduated in '83. She said this Lisa Oberman was here at the same time."

"What was the other name?"

"Tramell," said Nick. "Catherine Tramell."

She typed in the name and nodded as Catherine's name came up. "We have Tramell. But no Lisa Oberman."

Nick was puzzled. He could have sworn that Catherine had not been lying to him. Her fear and her disquiet about the memory of the obsessed Lisa Oberman had been too strong, too real for her to fake. Why would she lie about a thing like that? Like so much about Catherine Tramell, it just didn't make sense.

"There must be a Lisa Oberman," he

insisted to the student clerk. "Can there be some mistake?"

The woman looked at him coolly. "Only if you're making it," she said.

"Thanks," he said. "Thanks a lot."

"No problem," she said, turning back to her biology textbook.

Nick Curran drove directly to Catherine Tramell's house on Divisadero and saw her emerging with the slight, faded figure of Hazel Dobkins. Nick pulled to the curb and stood at the gate of the house.

Catherine did not seem nonplussed. "Hazel," she said calmly, "this is Nick. I told you all about him, do you remember?"

Hazel nodded and smiled distractedly. "You're the shooter, aren't you. How are you?"

It seemed to Nick that the old lady assumed they had something in common, a tie that bound them together, the fraternity of people who had taken a human life, as if they were members of an Elks' lodge. He half expected her to give him a killer's secret handshake.

"I'm fine," he said, "thank you." He turned to Catherine. "I need to speak to you for a minute."

Catherine directed Hazel toward the Lotus parked in front of the house. "Honey, why don't you get in the car? I'll be right there."

"Okay. Good-bye, Shooter," she said brightly.

When she was out of earshot, he turned back to Catherine, shaking his head. "You like to hang out with murderers or what? Did you know that Roxy—"

Catherine cut him off. "Of course I knew."

"And you didn't care? Or that made her all the more exotic. More desirable?"

"Look. I write about unusual people."

"Writing is one thing," he said. "Inviting them into your bed is another."

"Sometimes when I do my research, I get involved with them. It happens, you know."

"The hell it does."

"It happened with you," she said.

"It's not the same thing."

"Yes, it was. You were fascinated by me. I'm fascinated by killers. Killing isn't like smoking. You can quit."

"What the hell is that supposed to mean?"

She kissed him on the cheek, a warm, wifely sort of kiss. "I've got to go. I promised I'd get Hazel home by six o'clock. She just loves *America's Most Wanted*."

"What? She hopes to see someone she knew in the joint? Is that it?"

"I can't talk now," said Catherine, making for the car.

"There was no Lisa Oberman at Berkeley when you were there," he said, challenging her.

She stopped dead in her tracks. "What

were you doing? Checking up on me? What for?"

"Research," he said.

She slipped in behind the wheel of the Lotus and started the car. The window slipped down silently. "No Oberman, huh?"

"That's right."

"Well, why don't you try Lisa Hoberman?" She put the car in gear, gunned the engine a couple of times and then zoomed down the street.

The student who had dealt with Nick Curran at Berkeley's Dwinelle Hall was the same one who answered his call, placed hurriedly from a phone booth a few blocks away from Catherine's house. She recognized his voice; he recognized hers. Both pretended they had never spoke to one another before, though there was a detectable note of triumph in her manner. He *had* made a mistake, just as she supposed he had. Oberman, Hoberman—it was a trivial error and easy to make—but she felt vindicated nonetheless.

"Yeah," she said, "I have a Hoberman, Lisa, September 1979 to May 1983."

"Good," said Nick. He blocked the ear open to the sound of traffic on the street. "Give me all you've got."

"You want her grades?"

"Everything but her grades."

"I can tell you where she lived, I can tell

you her courses. Beyond that, there's not all that much."

He really didn't see the need to know how well Lisa Hoberman had done in school and ten-year-old information on her domiciles was useless. There was, however, one piece of information he could use, a nine-digit skeleton key to the lives of every American citizen.

"Do you have her social security number?" he asked.

"Yes." The student rattled off the number and he jotted it down in the notebook he kept in the back pocket of his pants.

"Thanks," he said. "I appreciate it."

Nick hung up and stood on the curb for a moment, pondering his next move. He wanted to know more about Lisa Hoberman and he knew where he could get further information. The problem was, he was denied access to the mainframe computers at police headquarters. He was sure that his computer password had been rendered inoperative and even if it hadn't, he couldn't afford to leave his name on the record. Whoever logged onto the machine had his name entered in the access file. Therefore, he required an accomplice, an accomplice who could keep his mouth shut.

The natural candidate was Gus Moran, of course, but Nick used up every curse and obscenity he knew listening to his partner's phone ring over and over again. Nick left the phone booth and checked the Wagon

Wheel and Mac's, finding both empty of
Gus.

That meant he'd have to go to the second
string. Andrews had helped him once before,
maybe he'd help him again. The detective
had not been happy about it, but Nick figured it was worth a shot.

Andrews was in the Ten-Four having a
couple of drinks with two other guys, whom
Nick recognized as cops, but didn't know by
name. They weren't Homicide, which was
a lucky break as they were unlikely to ask
questions about Nick's interest in talking to
Andrews. It was a sure bet, though, that
they knew all about Nick's troubles.

He got Andrews out of earshot of his
drinking buddies.

"Sam," he said, "I need a favor. . . ."

There was not a soul in the Homicide
squad room, which suited both of them just
fine. Andrews skulked around the big, clut-
tered office like a cat burglar, scarcely daring to breathe and turning on only a single
light.

"I must be out of my goddamn mind," he
muttered. "I could get my butt kicked but
good for this. Never mind opening files for
you, you're not even supposed to be in this
room. This goddamn building."

"I won't forget it, Sam, I really won't. I
never forget a favor."

"The only favor you'll be able to do me,
Nick, is get me a job at the same damn car-

wash you're gonna be working at. That's what we're both gonna be doing if we get caught here."

"Hey, don't knock it. It's probably a nice job. Out in the open, meet interesting people."

"Please," pleaded Andrews, "just shut up." He sat down at the computer terminal and logged on with his code.

"Good," whispered Nick, staring at the screen. "Run a Department of Motor Vehicles license check on Lisa Hoberman." He recited the social security number from memory.

Andrews tapped the information and the big brain settled for a moment, as if pondering the request. Then words flashed on the screen: 1987 Renewal—Elisabeth Garner. 147 Queenston Drive, Salinas, CA.

Nick almost cried out when he saw the name. Fighting a sickening, rising horror, he kept himself calm. "Bring up the license, will you Sam?"

Andrew issued the command and a computer-generated copy of the actual license appeared on the VDT screen. The photo on the document was undeniably that of the shrink whose life was so bound up in Nick's own.

"Hey!" said Andrews. "That's Doctor Garner, isn't it?"

"Yeah. Bring up 1980, please."

The ten-year-old picture was different, of course. Beth looked younger, less well-groomed—she had been a student at the time, after all. But that was not the most striking distinction about the photograph. The Beth Garner of today had dark brown hair, a lustrous chestnut color. The Beth Garner of ten years ago had blond hair, long golden tresses that Nick could see, even in a blurred license photograph, matched exactly the hair color of Catherine Tramell.

CHAPTER EIGHTEEN

Beth Garner didn't seem surprised to find Nick sitting in her darkened living room when she got back to her apartment that night. It was almost as if she was expecting his being there when she walked in. For his part, Nick was unapologetic about letting himself in.

"You shouldn't leave your door open. No telling who might drop in."

"I didn't leave the door open," she said coldly. "There's something wrong with the lock." She snapped on a light. "What do you want, Nick? I'm very tired."

"Tell me about Catherine."

She stared at him a moment, then shrugged. "She told you, didn't she? What did she tell you?"

"What did she tell me, Beth? Suppose I hear it from you, in your own words."

"I slept with her once, in school," she said briskly. As a psychologist, homosexuality was not abnormal behavior to her, nothing to be ashamed of. As a heterosexual though, she felt the need to justify her actions. "I was just a kid. I was experimenting. It was just that one time."

"Just once? You slept with her once and then you never saw her again. Is that it?"

Beth Garner hesitated a moment. "No ... no, it wasn't that simple. She developed a ... a fixation on me. She styled her hair like mine. She wore the same kind of clothes I did. She followed me around. She harassed me. Persecuted me. It was scary. It scared me then. It scares me now. She's a dangerous woman, Nick, you have to see that."

Nick nodded. It struck him that he was hearing mirror images of the same story. Beth Garner's words and her reaction to the incident were almost identical to Catherine Tramell's. The question was, who was the torturer and who was the victim.

"That's what she told you, isn't it?" asked Beth.

Nick shook his head. "No, not quite. She told me it was you."

"Me!"

"*You* wore the same kind of clothes as she did. *You* dyed your hair blond."

"I did dye my hair," Beth protested. "It didn't have anything to do with her. I was a redhead for a while, too. I told you, I was young, I was experimenting."

"Did you know Noah Goldstein?"

"I had him for two classes," said Beth.

Nick suddenly lost his temper. "You saw

all the reports on this case, Beth! Phil Walker had you copied on everything. You knew all about Catherine Tramell and you never said a damn thing. How the hell do you explain that?"

"What am I supposed to say?" Beth remonstrated. "What was I supposed to do? Go to you damn cops and say, 'Hey, I'm not gay or anything like that, guys, but it just so happens I *did* fuck your suspect ten years ago.'" She turned away, her arms crossed across her breasts, as if hugging herself for warmth. Tears glistened in the corners of her eyes. "It sounds crazy, it sounds hypocritical coming from me, a shrink, but I was embarrassed. It's the only time I've been with a woman."

"You think we would have been shocked? For God's sake, Beth, we're cops."

"Yeah, that's right—cops. The next thing you know it would have been all over the damn department. Little jokes, sniggering in the locker room." She gasped for breath trying to collect herself. "Anyway, that isn't important."

"What is, then?"

"The important thing, Nick, is that you watch out for her. She's really sick, you know? Don't you see what's going on here?" She stared at him, pleading with her eyes for understanding, begging with her gaze that he would believe her. "I don't know if she's playing out some kind of revenge thing here, but she's planned this whole thing.

She knows I went to Berkeley. She knows I knew Noah Goldstein. She makes up that story about me. She's trying to get you to think that I'm someone who's obsessed by her. She's trying to hand me over to you, tie a bow around me and say, 'Here's the psycho that killed Johnny Boz.' "

"She didn't hand you to me," said Nick furiously. "She doesn't know who you are. She told me about Lisa Hoberman. Not Beth Garner."

"I can't believe you'd be so stupid," retorted Beth. "She knew you'd find out who Lisa Hoberman is. You're a cop, after all—a good cop. What did she do? Let me guess. Tell you casually and make it sound irrelevant?" Beth smiled, but it was a twisted, nasty smile. "Did she tell you in bed, Nick? She must have. That's how I'd do it."

Nick turned away from her, remembering Catherine's shivering form as she recounted the terrifying story of Lisa Hoberman. "Why did you change your name, Beth?"

"I got married. He called me Beth."

"Married? I didn't know you were married."

"It was none of your business," she shot back. Then she shrugged, figuring that Nick might as well know everything. She was not ashamed of having been married and divorced. "I met my husband right out of med school. We interned together, he was on staff at the free clinic down in Salinas. The marriage didn't last long."

"How long?"

"Not long at all. Nick, do you really think I . . . that I could kill someone? I never even met Johnny Boz. Never even heard of him."

Nick's head was whirling. He didn't know who or what to believe anymore. He turned to go.

"What about Nilsen?" Beth called after him. "What possible motive would I have for killing Nilsen? It just doesn't add up. Nick, think about it."

Nick was thinking about it. He just wasn't talking about it, not to her, anyway. He fingered the broken dead bolt on her door. "You should do something about this lock, you know. Lot of bad elements around."

"That's right," said Beth fervidly. She held out her arms to him, as if to ward off some great satanic wickedness—a devilry she alone had the talismanic power to eradicate. "She's evil. She's brilliant. Be careful, Nick."

Nick nodded as if agreeing with her. But he had never been careful, not about anything and *never* about women. Why start now?

He was not careful when he entered the darkened lobby of his apartment building, and he didn't think twice about trudging up the dimly lit stairway to his front door. While he was digging his keys out of his pocket, he felt a hand on his shoulder and he jumped as if scalded.

"Jesus Christ!"

Catherine Tramell had emerged from the shadows and was laughing at him.

"Did I scare you?" she asked, her eyes bright with merriment. She knew full well she had frightened him and somehow that seemed to please her—just as it had when she had jumped him on the beach.

"You should never sneak up on a man you know to be armed," he said. "That's how accidents happen."

"But I know you're not armed," she said. "You had to have handed over your gun when you went . . . on leave."

She was right, of course. He touched the place under his left arm where his .38 would normally have nestled. Carrying a gun had become second nature to him. Now he felt undressed without it.

"Anyway, I just thought I'd surprise you," she said, her voice lively, almost chipper. Then she saw something was bothering him, something more troubling than her taking him by surprise. "What's the matter, Nick?"

"I found Lisa Hoberman," he said.

"You did? What's she doing?"

"Just interested in what your old college pal is up to, is that it?"

She stared at him a moment, disbelieving. "You mean, you're not going to tell me what she's doing? I thought we weren't playing games anymore."

Nick unlocked the door of his apartment, but didn't enter, standing in the doorway, as if barring the entrance. "I did, too. I thought that the games were a thing of the past."

"They are," she insisted.

"Then how is it that the story I hear is a little different from yours? She told me things were the other way around—that you were obsessed with her. She said you even styled your hair the way *she* did."

Catherine smiled slowly. "And you believed her? Your capacity for gullibility astonishes me, Nick, it really does. I was the victim there. I was the one who had to go down to the campus police and make out a report about her."

"You did?" He still didn't believe her.

"That's right. You still think I kill people, don't you?"

Nick didn't think she killed people. He didn't *want* to think her capable of it. "No," he said quietly.

"Liar," she spat, turning on her heel and walking back down the murky stairs with the aplomb and self-assurance of a *haut couture* model.

CHAPTER NINETEEN

One of the great things about being on leave, Nick thought as he waited in his car to cross the Bay Bridge, was that the caseload was so much lighter. Normally, he and Gus were working a half a dozen homicides simultaneously, just fighting to keep abreast of the details of each investigation. Now, on psycho leave, Nick was free to devote his time to a single case, the one that interested him most: unraveling the twisted life of Catherine Tramell. It wasn't even about Johnny Boz anymore. Now Nick wanted to know *her*, separate the lies from the truths, the fact from the fiction.

He cruised over the bridge to Berkeley that morning, parking his car on Bancroft and making his way onto the campus. In front of the massive Doe Memorial Library he ran into a Berkeley campus cop who told him that the headquarters of the University Security could be found in the basement of Colton Hall.

The campus policeman at the desk was a middle-aged man, an ex-cop who would have spent most of the morning boring Nick with stories of his days on the Albany police force, had not Nick impressed upon him the urgency of his mission. He spoke to the old guy as if he were a real cop, a brother-in-arms.

"I have to get back to San Francisco with the file," said Nick, "or the lieutenant will have my ass. You know how it is."

The old man chuckled. "Sure do. We had some real pains in the ass in my day too, you know."

"I bet."

The campus cop led him into the university security records room. It was stacked floor to ceiling with old folders, one for every incident reported in the modern history of the University of California, Berkeley. Among the accounts of panty raids and beer bashes that got out of hand, were the more serious crimes.

"What did you say you were with?" asked the campus cop.

"Homicide," said Nick.

"The homicide guys I met were always hotshots. You a hotshot?"

"Nope," said Nick.

"Glad to hear it." The man had stopped at one of the file drawers and extracted a folder. "Here we go," he said, glancing at the yellowed dossier. "Sort of."

"How do you mean, sort of?"

"There was a report about Lisa Hoberman—January 1980. But it's not here. It's
out."

"Out? What is this? A library?" demanded
Nick.

The campus cop looked at him disapprov-
ingly, as if beginning to suspect that Nick
Curran was, after all, nothing more than a
homicide hotshot. "Simmer down, mister."

"Who's got it?"

"One of your guys. Fella by the name of
Nilsen."

Nick tore the paper from the man's hands
and read the single line: On Loan to SFPD
Det. M. Nilsen. Internal Affairs 11/19/90.

"Know the guy?" asked the campus cop.

"Yeah," said Nick slowly. "I know him."

"Well, tell him we want it back. He's had
it a whole year, you know."

"Yeah," said Nick. "I'll be sure to tell
him."

Nick's head was spinning and he needed
a good-sized dose of clear thinking administered by Doctor Gus Moran. He called his
partner from a public phone on the Berkeley
campus and they arranged to meet on the
San Francisco side of the bay. Wanting some
place nice and discreet, they chose the fog-
enshrouded Pier 7, south of Market and the
Embarcadero. They paced the long, disused
dock going over the facts again and again.

"So Nilsen had a report on her, so what?

You don't know what the hell was in it,"
said Gus.

"Catherine *told* me what was in it."

"*If* she was telling the truth," cautioned
Gus.

"Don't you get it, Gus? If Beth killed
Johnny Boz to frame Catherine, she wouldn't
want anyone to know what had happened at
Berkeley, even if it was years ago. But
Nilsen found out about it. And that gave
Beth a clear motive to kill him."

"Yeah," said Gus like a debater, "but how
the hell did Nilsen find out about it? If it
happened, that is."

"He was Internal Affairs. He probably
asked her about it."

Gus thought about this a moment. Something didn't make sense to him. "But she'd
have to be nuttier than a twenty-pound
Christmas fruitcake. And Beth Garner's not
the one who hangs out with multiple murderers. Now your girlfriend, on the other
hand, she's got real cozy with a couple of
'em."

"She's a writer," Nick said defensively.
"It's part of what she does. Research."

"Maybe I'll buy that lame excuse," said
Gus. "Maybe not. Haven't made up my
mind yet. It sure would be easier if we could
find out what the hell happened at Berkeley
back then. There's gotta be *somebody* who
knows what the hell happened."

"I *know* what happened," Nick insisted.

"Catherine told me. And everything she's said has checked out."

"You got goddamn tweety birds flutterin' around your head, that's what you've got."

"The hell I do."

Gus grinned. "Do you really think you and she are gonna fuck like minks, raise rug rats and live happily ever after? *Oh man!* Please don't tell your old pal Gus that's what you're thinking."

That was sort of what Nick was thinking, but not even he could bring himself to say it to Gus. "I don't know what the hell to think," he said quietly.

"Good," said Gus. "There's hope for you yet."

"Look," said Nick, "there's gotta be a way to get to the bottom of this. Like you said, someone has to know something."

"Well, maybe we oughta do like your girlfriend does, a little research. I'm gonna concentrate on her, find someone who can fill in some of the blanks."

"How you gonna do that?"

"Just so happens, sonny, that I am a trained police professional. Lucky break for us, huh?"

Nick smiled. "You go after her. I'm going after Beth."

"Big mistake."

"Maybe, but there are some things that have to be checked out."

"Bet I'm right and you're wrong," said Gus confidently.

"That's a bet I'll take."

Gus nodded. "I'll meet you right here, on this old pier in twenty-four hours. You'll see, sonny, you'll see that your old partner ain't quite ready for pasture yet."

Nick climbed the stairs to his apartment, mindful of who or what might be lurking in the shadows. There was no one there, but as he clambered up the steps he noticed that he heard music—and it seemed to be coming from his apartment. He stopped at the door and listened. It was coming from inside. Gingerly, he put his head around the door and peeked in.

Catherine was standing by the window. She wore black jeans and her beloved black leather motorcycle jacket, zipped almost to the neck.

"I couldn't stay mad at you," she said. "I missed you."

"I wasn't gone long enough for you to miss me," he said gruffly.

"Did you miss *me*?"

"No."

Her lips formed a little moue. "Come over here and tell me no."

He walked up close to her, and stared into her eyes. "No," he said. "I didn't miss you."

Very slowly, she began to unzip her motorcycle jacket. As the teeth parted, it became apparent that she wore nothing beneath the heavy leather.

"I've seen 'em before," said Nick.

"But you might not see them again. My book is almost finished. And the detective is nearly dead."

"Really? Does he have time for a last cigarette?"

She pulled him close. "Afterward," she said huskily.

They made love quickly and hungrily on the floor of his living room. The intense attraction they felt for each other surged through their bodies, hot and fast, like molten metal.

When they were done, he fumbled in his pants for his cigarettes, fished one out of the crumpled pack, sucked down a lungful of smoke and then passed it to her.

"I have to do some research tomorrow," he said.

"I'm very good at research. I'll help you."

He reclaimed the cigarette from her and took a drag on it. "No thanks."

"What are you researching?"

"A new ending for your book."

Catherine smiled. "Really? What's the twist?"

"The twist is, the detective doesn't die. Him and the wrong girl."

"What happens to them?"

"It's a happy ending."

"I hate happy endings."

"I figured. But try this one out."

She snatched the cigarette from his lips and puffed. "Okay, try me."

"Him and the wrong girl, they fuck like

minks, raise rug rats and live happily ever after."

Catherine considered this for a moment. "It won't sell," she said finally.

"Why not?"

"Because somebody has to die."

"Why?"

"Because somebody always does," she said.

CHAPTER TWENTY

Salinas is the county seat of Monterey, a drab little town just inland from the spectacular Monterey coastline, but as different from the chic little coastal towns as you can get. Salinas makes its money from the giant vegetable farms that ring it and from the food-processing plants in the industrial section of town. On every street corner, you'll find migrant farm workers hoping for employment, and the air is tinged with the smells from the big McCormick spice plant on the eastern edge of the city.

Salinas was the only place Nick could think of going to for information on Beth Garner. She had said that she had been married here and her husband had worked at the Salinas clinic. Maybe her ex-husband knew something and if he did, Nick was determined to get it out of him.

The free clinic catered to the migrant labor force and Nick found it on the edge of town, close to the fields and the railroad tracks.

The emergency room was half filled with patients waiting their turn to see a doctor, but Nick himself was not in the mood to wait. He went straight to the nurses' station. There were two of them, both in their late twenties. Both were immersed in paperwork.

"Hi," he said to one. "I'm looking for a Doctor Garner. Could you tell me where to find him?"

"We don't have a Doctor Garner on staff at the clinic, sir."

"You don't?"

"We did. Some time ago, when I first started here. Doctor Joseph Garner."

"That would be him," said Nick.

"Well, I'm afraid he's no longer with us."

"Do you know where he went?"

"No, you don't understand. He is no longer with us. With anybody. He died."

"Died? How did he die?"

The nurse hesitated a moment. "He was shot. And that's all I know about it."

Nick found one of the deputy sheriffs of Salinas standing out in front of the police station, hosing down a white Chevy Blazer. It wasn't a police vehicle and the cop seemed to have plenty of time to wash his own car and jaw with the cop from the big city. He knew all about the death of Doctor Joseph Garner.

He directed a sharp spray of water across the windshield. "Doctor Garner, damndest thing. This is a pretty quiet town. Not a lot of trouble with the migrant workers. They know if they cause trouble they'll get sent back." Water thrummed on the side door panel of the truck.

"And Garner? What about him?"

"Like I say, it was strange. He was walking home from work. Him and his wife lived only a couple of blocks from the clinic. Somebody just drove by and shot him."

"A driveby?" said Nick. "What is this, Oakland?"

"Nope. It's pretty strange, like I said."

"What was the weapon?"

"Thirty-eight revolver. Never recovered." He directed the hose at the tires, the water blasting mud off the hubcaps.

"Were there ever any suspects?"

"Nope. No suspects, no motive. Unsolved."

"Was his wife ever a suspect?"

The sheriff cut off the jet of water and regarded Nick curiously. "You know, I had another one of you guys down here from Frisco, 'bout a year ago. He asked me the same question. What's this about, anyway?"

"Routine," said Nick, which they both knew was cop code for "mind your own business."

"Yeah, he said it was routine, too. Now it's two guys saying it was routine."

"Do you remember his name?"

The sheriff thought for a moment, then shook his head. "Nope, can't say that I do."

"If you heard it, would you recognize it?"

"Might." He turned on the hose again, concentrating on the back tires now.

"Nilsen?"

"That's him."

"*Was* she ever a suspect?"

The cop shook his head. "Nope. There was talk. It never panned out, though."

"What kind of talk?" Nick persisted.

"A girlfriend," said the sheriff.

"He had a girlfriend?"

"Nope. *She* did. But like I say, it never panned out." He turned off the hose and started coiling it. The Chevy gleamed and dripped.

"Thanks," said Nick.

"Hope I helped you out."

"You did," said Nick. "You did."

There was another sound at Catherine's house on Stinson Beach. Another sound as regular and as rhythmic as the pounding of the surf. It was the sound of the laser printer of her word processor, shooting out pages of her book.

The machine was so quiet that Nick wasn't aware of it until he was well inside the house. There was no sign of Catherine, but someone had taken the first sheaf of printed pages out of the tray. He picked up the top one, a title page. It read: *Shooter* by Catherine Woolf.

"You like the title?" She was standing in the doorway.

"Very . . . catchy," he said.

"It's finished. I finished my book."

He riffled the pages. "How does it end?"

"I told you. She kills him." She ground out her cigarette. "Good-bye, Nick."

"Good-bye?"

"I finished my book." The words did not seem to have any effect on Nick. He stood rooted to the spot. "Didn't you hear me?"

Nick gave no sign of having heard. He stared at her, searching her face for a sign, some symbol of reconciliation.

"Your character is dead, Nick. That means good-bye." She started back out toward the terrace. "What do you want, Nick, flowers? I'll send you an autographed copy. How's that?"

"What is this—some kind of joke?" He almost smiled, sure that he was finally able to figure her out. "Are we playing games again?"

"The games are over," she said sternly. "You were right. It was the fuck of the century, Shooter."

"What the hell are you talking about?"

From inside the house someone called. "Catherine?" It was an old voice, the call of an old lady.

"I'll be right there, Hazel," Catherine replied. " 'Bye, Nick," she said quietly.

"But—"

"I mean it," she said. And there was something in her voice that told him that she wasn't, for once, playing games.

*   *   *

Nick got to the pier before Gus. He waited in his car, smoking. Gus pulled his Cadillac up alongside the Mustang and hit the horn. He leaned over and opened the passenger-side door of the big old car.

"Get in," he yelled to Nick.

Nick slid in next to his partner and could tell just by the look on Gus's face that the older cop had something, something pretty big. Gus fairly radiated excitement.

"I got a lot of stuff might interest you, sonny. I've been phoning people from Tramell's dorm. Went and got her yearbook, got the alumni association on it, everything. They're very helpful, those folks over in Berkeley."

"Great," Nick said sourly. "C'mon, Gus, hurry up."

"Don't rush me, sonny. So word gets around and this morning I get a phone call from Catherine Tramell's roommate her freshman year—"

"*She* called *you*?"

"That's right. Name of Mary Beth Lambert. I look her up in the yearbook and that's her all right. She says she knows all about Catherine Tramell and Lisa Hoberman. I'll tell you, that girlfriend of yours has always had a knack for spooking people. All this time later, this Mary Beth Lambert, she says she doesn't want to talk about Catherine on the phone. Insists on doing it face to face— said I could be anybody. She's over in Oakland, gonna meet her at work in her office on Pill Hill. She said it would be better that way, after hours, after all her co-workers have split for the day. That's what she said, 'split.'" Gus started the car. "Feel like a ride to Oakland, sonny?"

Nick just shrugged. If Catherine had really cut him out of her life—if he *really* had been nothing more than research—then he didn't feel like doing anything.

"You look lousy, son," said Gus. "Don't feel bad about ol' Gus beating you. I had to go out on a high note. Let an old man have a little bit of glory. You got a problem with that?"

"I don't have a problem with that, Gus," Nick said softly.

"Good." He gunned the car into the traffic making for the Bay Bridge and the East Bay. He was still bubbling over his discoveries. "And the roommate isn't all I found. Did you know Beth Garner has a private practice? She shares an office on Van Ness with another headshrinker. And do you know who her officemate's star patient is? Or rather, was? *Johnny-fuckin'-Boz!*" Gus whooped and pounded the steering wheel. "Catherine Tramell knows this and figures she can set it up that Beth is some psycho with an ice pick. You lose, son, you lose!" He glanced over at Nick, expecting to see him squirming and all ready with some obscene comeback. But Nick sat stock still, his face set in stone.

It wasn't like him to be a sore loser. "What the hell's the matter with you?"

"Shut up, Gus."

Gus shrugged. "Sorry I spoke." They rode the rest of the way to Oakland in silence.

Pill Hill was in North Oakland—a cluster of office buildings and hospitals, the medical hub of the East Bay. Gus wheeled the Caddy to a halt in front of one building, an office tower, and parked. Both men got out of the car.

"Where the hell you going?" asked Gus.

"I'm going with you."

"Uh-uh. You're on leave, son. This won't take long. I'll be back in a minute."

"Well, will you at least tell me where you're going?"

"Suite 405, son. Just wait in the car till I get back. Then we'll go have a couple of drinks and I'll tell you the whole story."

Nick hesitated a moment.

"This is my story, Nick, let me handle it."

Nick nodded. "Okay." He got back into the car and Gus started toward the building.

The office tower was deserted, but the building was unlocked and the doors of the elevator stood open on the ground floor. Gus got in and punched the button for the fourth floor. The car rose one floor and stopped, the doors sweeping open.

Gus hit the button again and cursed under his breath. The elevator rose and stopped at the third floor. The doors opened to an empty hall.

"Goddamn!" Gus hated technology. The doors closed again and the elevator ascended.

The doors swept open at four and Gus emerged into the shadowy corridor. He wasn't expecting to see anyone so he only caught a glimpse of long blond hair and the flash of an ice pick. He saw it glimmer just before it struck him in the throat.

Nick sat slumped in the front seat of the car when suddenly something Gus said struck him with the force of an uppercut. Catherine's freshman year roommate called him. What were the chances of that happening? Someone called Gus and lured him straight into a trap—it had to be!

Nick burst out of the car, blasting toward the building. He went up the stairs three at a time and exploded through the steel fire door on the fourth floor.

Gus was crumpled in the open door of the elevator, blood streaming from a dozen wounds in his neck, his jowls, his cheeks, and his face. The door tried to close, and struck Gus's bleeding body and pulled open again.

"Gus!" Nick screamed. He dropped on his knees to his fallen partner and tried to staunch the flow of blood with his bare hands. The warm fluid flowed through his fingers in a sticky torrent.

Gus's eyes were glazed over, life was slipping out of him second by second. Death rattled in his throat.

"Gus, Gus," moaned Nick, "No, *please*."

Gus shuddered and slumped. Nick was soaked in his partner's blood. He tore the gun from Gus's waist. The elevator was stopped and Nick had not seen anyone on the stairs. Whoever killed Gus was still there, on the floor.

A noise, Nick swiveled around and came face to face with exactly the person he was expecting.

"Freeze!" Nick yelled, holding the gun out in front of him in the combat stance. The muzzle was trained squarely on Beth Garner's chest.

She blanched white and recoiled, her hands darting into the pockets of her raincoat. "What are you doing here?"

"Put your hands up!"

"Where's Gus? I got a message on my machine to meet Gus here. Where is he?"

She was holding something in the right pocket of her coat. "Put your fucking hands up!" Nick screamed. "Don't move!"

"Nick, please—" She advanced a pace.

"Don't! Don't move!" He cocked the gun. "I know about your husband."

Beth seemed to pale even more. "My husband?"

"And I know you liked girls. You still like girls, Beth?"

"*What*?" She smiled strangely, a weird, understanding smile and took another step toward him.

"Take your hands out of your pockets!"

"What is the matter with you?" She stormed toward him, her hand coming out of her pocket as she came.

Nick fired once, the report of the gun loud in the room. The bullet slammed into her chest, throwing her back and down to the floor.

He kept the gun on her a moment. Beth was still alive—barely. He dropped to one knee and pulled her right hand from her pocket. Clasped tightly in her fist were her keys. No gun.

Beth whispered something so low and soft that he had to bend down till his ear was almost resting on her lips.

She murmured her last words. "I loved you."

"What made you think she had a gun?" Phil Walker stood over Nick Curran, confused and concerned. Gus Moran was dead, Beth Garner was dead, and Nick Curran seemed to have turned into a zombie. The crime-scene gang ranged around him—the coroners, the IA guys, the uniforms—but Nick's eyes hardly registered the hustle and bustle.

"What the hell was Beth doing here? What was Gus doing here?" Phil Walker was desperate for some answers, but talking to Nick was like talking to an inanimate object. "What the hell were *you* doing here?"

Sam Andrews tapped Walker on the shoulder. "Got something, Lieutenant."

"What?"

A forensics man was holding a raincoat in his gloved hands. "Found it in the stairwell up on five. It's got fresh bloodstains on it and there's a blond wig and an ice pick in the pocket."

"Ice pick?"

The forensics guy pulled the pick from the pocket. "Yeah," he said. "And check this." He folded the raincoat inside out. Stitched into the lining were the initials: SFPD.

Walker swept a hand through his hair. "Jesus."

There wasn't much more to see at the building in Oakland, so the whole team moved across the bay to San Francisco, to Beth Garner's apartment in the Marina district. They swarmed into the dwelling, storming through the place like a group of Marines taking a beach. Nick wandered in after them, thinking of something Gus had once said to him. Nick could hear his partner's gravelly voice as clearly as if he was standing there—"Don't get yourself murdered, Nick, you'll get no privacy if you do."

"Lieutenant?" called Andrews. "We found a gun. A .38 revolver. In the bookcase, behind some books."

"Have ballistics check it for Nilsen," ordered Walker.

"There's something else."

"What?"

"Photographs," said Andrew. "Photographs of Catherine Tramell."

This seemed to get Nick's attention. He joined Walker as he walked into the bedroom. The top of Beth's dresser seemed to be a shrine to Catherine Tramell. There were copies of her books and stacks of photographs of her—Catherine in college, Catherine at a fight, Catherine with Johnny Boz, Catherine with Roxy.

Walker turned to Nick. "Well, I guess that's it," he said.

Deep in the night, Walker's team assembled at the Homicide Bureau, the offices a hive of activity. Talcott had ordered that the whole case had to be wrapped, nice and neat, by dawn. He was planning on holding a news conference, he said, and he didn't want any loose ends.

The raincoat and the blond wig were lying on a desk. "It's her size. It's Gus's blood," said Andrews.

"She must have heard you coming," said Walker to Nick, "and dumped the stuff."

Andrews read from his notes. "There was no suite 405 in that building. Catherine Tramell's roommate in her freshman year is dead. She died of leukemia two years ago. We're getting a fax of her death certificate."

"Anything else?"

"Yep," said Andrews. "This is the big

one. Ballistics says the .38 we found in her apartment was used on Nilsen. No registration. They're checking it against the one used on her husband in Salinas. The ice pick is the same model used on Johnny Boz."

Nick did not appear to have heard. He was still in a daze—and, deep down, relieved that Catherine was in the clear.

"Is there a connection between her and Boz?"

Andrews nodded. "Yeah. Johnny Boz's psychiatrist said that he introduced them at a Christmas party at his house about a year ago. Said they really hit it off."

Walker patted Nick Curran on the shoulder. "You just can't tell about people, can you? Even the ones you think you know inside out."

That wasn't the only pat on the back Nick got that night. Talcott swallowed his pride and shook Nick's hand.

"Congratulations, Curran," he said through clenched teeth.

CHAPTER TWENTY-ONE

Despite Talcott's intention to hold a carefully scripted news conference the next morning, word of the break in the killings had gotten out. It had been broadcast on the twenty-four hour news services and heard only by the insomniacs, night owls, and news junkies—and Catherine Tramell.

She was waiting at the door of Nick's apartment when he finally came home. She wore no makeup. She looked young, freshfaced, vulnerable, and worried.

He stared at her, expressionless.

"I can't allow myself," she said, "I can't allow myself to care about you. I can't allow myself to care. I can't—I can't."

Nick moved toward her and put his arms around her, holding her close.

There were tears in her eyes. "I don't want to do this. Please. I don't want to do this. I lose everybody. I don't want to lose you. I don't want to . . ."

He pressed her closer, guiding her into his

apartment and into his bedroom. Gently he removed her clothes and laid her carefully on the bed, bending to kiss her face, then her breasts. Her arms snaked up behind his neck and pulled him down to her, thrusting her bare body against his.

Then he was atop her, making love to her, gently, tenderly, scarcely moving inside of her. The little bit of light in the room caught the tears in her eyes and they glistened.

They came together, soft waves of pleasure breaking over them, a swell of sexual bliss that carried them through the silent, dark minutes of the night.

Later they lay quietly, next to each other on the bed. Nick's gaze was fixed on the ceiling as smoke from his cigarette drifted slowly upward.

Catherine was curled away from him, her face hidden.

"What do we do now, Nick?"

After a pause, he answered, "We fuck like minks. We raise rug rats. We live happily ever after."

"I hate rug rats," she said.

"We fuck like minks. We forget the rug rats. We live happily ever after."

Catherine slipped further over on her side, her hair tumbling over the edge of the bed, her hands dangling, touching the floor. Her face was suddenly expressionless. She turned and met his gaze directly.

"I love you," she whispered and kissed him passionately, urgently.

She pushed him down on his back, sitting astride him, her breasts high and taut. She leaned down and kissed him again, her hair closing around their faces like a golden curtain. She kissed him deep, wet, and hot. Nick pushed Catherine over onto her back and entered her with one smooth, strong motion.

Nick thought only of that moment's pleasure; his body's need. He was completely, blissfully unaware of the thin, steel-handled ice pick which lay hidden under the bed.

SIGNET

Published or forthcoming

FADE THE HEAT

Jay Brandon

Mark Blackwell is District Attorney of San Antonio, city of favours and pay-offs. His success has cost him his marriage and family life. Now his son stands accused of rape.

During the trial that follows Mark is torn apart, caught in the judicial wheel that he has set in motion. As the pressure builds, the media and his rivals move in for the kill. Suddenly he has everything to lose and nothing to gain...

'A clever plot, a gripping novel' – Tony Hillerman, author of *Talking God*

'Tension radiates from every page ... guilty of being an enthralling read' – *Today*

Published or forthcoming

THE RATING GAME

Dave Cash

Behind the glass-fronted walls of CRFM's 24-hours-a-day nerve centre in the heart of London, three people fight for control of their lives as the tycoon powerbrokers of international finance move in for the kill...

Monica Hammond, the radio station's beautiful and ruthless Managing Director – nothing was allowed to stand in her way ... until one man discovered her fatal weakness.

Nigel Beresford-Clarke – CRFM's greatest asset – hopelessly betrayed by his love for a schoolgirl...

And **Maggie Lomax**, uncompromising and tough as nails – then her outspoken broadcasts pushed the wrong people too far ...

They're ready to play ... *The Rating Game*

SIGNET

Published or forthcoming

HAVING IT ALL

Maeve Haran

Having it All. Power. Money. Success. *And* a happy family. Liz really believed she could have it all. So when she's offered one of the most important jobs in television, she jumps at it.

But Liz discovers that there's a price to be paid for her success and that the whole glittering image is just an illusion. And one day she's faced with the choice she thought she'd never have to make.

Liz decides she *will* have it all – but on her own terms.

'Will touch cords, tug heartstrings. Every woman's been here' – Penny Vincenzi, author of *Old Sins*

'Realistic, compassionate, but still as paccy as they come' – *Cosmopolitan*

SIGNET

Published or forthcoming

Ira Levin
author of *Rosemary's Baby*

Thirteen hundred Madison Avenue, an elegant 'sliver' building, soars high and narrow over Manhattan's smart Upper East Side. Kay Norris, a successful single woman, moves on to the twentieth floor of the building, high on hopes of a fresh start and the glorious Indian summer outside. But she doesn't know that someone is listening to her. Someone is *watching* her.

'Levin really knows how to touch the nerve ends' – *Evening Standard*

'*Sliver* is the ultimate *fin de siècle* horror novel, a fiendish goodbye-wave to trendy urban living ... Ira Levin has created the apartment dweller's worst nightmare' – Stephen King

ADENYDD A CHADWYNI